Lake Shore

AWAKENING

A REDEMPTION SHORES NOVEL

JENNIFER RODEWALD

Rooted Publishing

McCook, NE 69001

Email: jen@authorjenrodewald.com

https://authorjenrodewald.com/

CONTENTS

CHAPTER ONE

FORTY-TWO MORE DAYS UNTIL "I do"... Joy bubbled in Janie's heart as she flipped through her bridal magazine. An unrepentant grin stretched her mouth—one that hadn't faded, it seemed, since Thanksgiving—as she looked forward to the coming weekend.

They would be working on the final touches at the Splendor. Pending everything passed inspection, not only would they have the wedding of their hopes there, but she and Hunter would spend their first week as husband and wife as the lodge's first guests.

Giggling at that little secret, she replayed Hunter's sly grin when they'd mapped out a plan to sneak back to the lodge after their wedding guests disappeared.

Janie glanced down at the speck of a diamond resting on her left ring finger. The same one she'd worn eight years ago. Hunter had promised that he'd buy her a bigger diamond—a better ring. She'd given him an emphatic *no*. She wanted this ring. The one he'd given her when they'd been little more than kids. Wearing it now was like wearing redemption. She didn't want bigger, shinier, or more expensive.

She wanted the love they'd grown back then. Returned, restored, and ready for that forever they'd promised. How glorious was that?

Biting her bottom lip, she rolled her fingers, lifted her arms, and wiggled her hands while she turned a little happy dance in her kitchen.

This weekend would be the first of a lifetime of working side by side at the lodge. They would finish the trim work, paint the guest rooms, and for the first time ever, she would employ that gorgeous new kitchen.

Woo-hoo!

The bell at the front of the café jingled moments before she stepped into another happy jig.

Janie contained her excitement just enough to not appear ridiculous as she strode into the dining room.

Tame the giddiness, girl. It might be . . .

A release of nervous adrenaline tingled through her arms. Her heart stuttered before she glimpsed the young woman—a stranger—who wandered inside the café.

Not Grady. Where had that guy been? She knew he'd been back to Luna in the months since their misadventures in Utah. And he'd promised he'd stop by the café.

But he hadn't. Guilt ate at Janie's joy with every passing week that Grady didn't show up. And with that, a growing anxiety about the time she would see him again. Today was not that day.

Relief washed down from the hairs on her head clear to her toes.

Her lungs emptied with relief as she inspected the young woman drawing up to the pine slab counter. Blue eyes and dark hair, not even twenty years old. By the looks of it, barely old enough to drive. Maybe. The girl wore an inquiring expression—though there was a secretiveness about her.

"Hi there." Janie wiped her hands on her apron and approached the young woman from her side of the counter. She glanced out the big window, half expecting to see an adult trail the girl. "It's a little cold out there, isn't it?"

The girl brushed the white flakes of melting snow from the shoulders of her white coat. "Yeah. Especially to a girl from Austin. It's full-on spring down there."

"Texas?" Janie chuckled as she glanced outside again. Big white flakes drifted toward the already piled and packed snowdrifts that lined Luna's Main Street. Was this kid alone? All the way from Texas? "You flew north during the wrong season, sweetie. We're still in the clutches of winter up here." Looking back at the pretty thing, she winked. "Can I get you something to warm up with? Coffee? Or I make a sonnet-worthy raspberry hot cocoa, if you're up for near death in a good way."

Those pensive eyes crinkled at the side with a small grin. "Death in a good way? Never heard of that. But now that I have, I must try it. And the warmer, the better." She shivered dramatically. "I've worn flip-flops every day of my life. This place is positively artic."

Janie chuckled. "Artic? Yikes. This is a decent March day in Luna. One almost-scalding drink coming your way." She turned for her drink bar and pulled down a clean mug. "What brings you to Montana, miss flip-flops from Texas?"

The sound of a barstool scraping against the wood floor preceded the girl's response. "It's . . . personal."

Huh. Personal in Luna, Montana? There was a mystery that promised to be town gossip within the week.

Janie stirred the steamed milk and dark chocolate until the drink was a yummy frothy brown color. She added her homemade wild raspberry syrup and topped the liquid with a generous helping of whipped cream, then sprinkled thin chocolate shavings over the white peak. Full mug in hand, she placed the drink in front of her guest. "See if this doesn't warm your southern soul."

That earned her a half smile, though the wariness remained on the girl's face.

"Did you come all this way alone?" Janie couldn't help but ask.

Looking at the counter, the girl took a long sip, wiped her mouth with a napkin, and then glanced around the empty café before she finally looked back at Janie. She shrugged.

"Seems like quite a trip for a single girl." How old was this kid anyway? Sixteen?

"I made it."

"I see that." Janie leaned her hip against the counter. "Sweetie, are you okay?"

"I'm fine." That came too fast. And her eyes fell back to the counter.

"How old are you?"

"Old enough to drive."

An answer a teenager would give. Janie paused in the midst of her whirling thoughts—one of which was to contact Jeremy Yates and see what he thought of this kid on her own and over a thousand miles from home.

Lord, I need some wisdom here.

This was becoming a refreshing, revived habit, seeking God's help. Briefly, Janie wondered why she'd abandoned that practice in the first place. She didn't have to wonder too hard—anger, bitterness, guilt, regret—the silent killers of a spiritual life . . . They'd all become a wedge between her heart and her heavenly Father's.

What a grace it was that God had seen fit to pluck those obstacles away—even though she'd been the one to push them there in the first place. Hopefully, she'd learn to do better with challenging situations—to ask God for guidance rather than follow the bluster of her impulsive emotions.

Guidance right now would be good . . .

Hazel. Think of this girl like you'd think of Hazel. Independent. Skittish. And quite possibly wounded.

Janie tried for a casual countenance as she crossed her arms. "How long will you be in town?"

"Maybe I'm just passing through." Sass tinged her tone.

"Passing through Luna in March?" Janie dropped her hands to her hips. "I've lived here my whole life, sweetie. I can tell you for a fact that doesn't happen this time of year. If you land in Luna in the deep freeze of winter, you did it on purpose."

Those tight shoulders rolled in a little more as her jaw tightened.

"Maybe I can help, hmm?"

The girl peeked at Janie.

Pressing her arms to the counter, Janie leaned closer. "This is a small town, and we all know who is who and usually what they're up to. I can promise you're safe here, as far as other people go. But the winter"—she nodded toward the window—"you already know. It's cold. Nights are bitter. Do you have a place to stay?"

Another shrug.

Realization stalled Janie's heart. "You can't sleep in your car, sweetie. You'll freeze."

"I can too. I'll leave the heater running."

"Then you'll suffocate. Carbon monoxide." Janie reached toward the kid and touched her arm. "Let me help you."

"I don't even know you."

Janie stood straight. "You're right. I'm Janie Truitt, and this my café."

The girl's head jolted up, and as she met Janie's look, her eyes sparked with . . . something. Hope? She studied Janie for several heartbeats as the wariness seeped back into her gaze. Then she nodded. "Olivia."

Olivia . . . who? Janie bit her bottom lip and weighed how much to press. Again, she thought of Hazel and decided not to push too much. Skittish creatures required delicate persistence.

"You own this place?"

Surprised that Olivia spoke again, Janie nodded. "I do."

"Must be nice."

"Usually. It's a lot of work—super early mornings, sometimes some late nights. But this was my dream." One that Janie still cherished. But she was working out a new plan—a new dream. One that included Hunter and his lodge and a way she could be a part of that and still keep the café. That part was complicated.

Please, God, help us work this out together this time . . .

"I mean it must be nice to have something of your own. Did you get it from your family?"

An odd question. Janie pulled her brows together. "As a matter of fact, it was my aunt's."

"On your dad's side?"

What in the world? "No. My mom's aunt—so my great-aunt."

"Oh." Olivia looked into her mug, a scowl creasing her face.

"What about you? What do you do in Texas?"

"Do?"

"Do you have a job?"

"I—" She pinned her lips tight.

"I see." Janie crossed her arms again and leaned against the counter. "You're still in high school, aren't you?"

No answer. Not even a glance up.

"What grade?"

"Why do you care?"

"I'm a little worried about a high school student from Texas driving herself clear up to Luna, Montana, without a place to stay or someone to help her."

"Who says I need help?"

Tipping her head to one side, Janie waited for Olivia to glance up, and wasn't a bit surprised to see defiance in her expression.

"Okay." Janie shrugged and slid her hands into her apron pocket. "That'll be five fifty."

"Wh . . . what?"

"Your hot chocolate. It's five dollars and fifty cents."

"Oh." Olivia leaned so she could dig into the pockets of her ripped skinny jeans. She pulled out a wad of cash—mostly ones—and milled through the bills.

Janie counted silently as she watched Olivia prepare to pay. She had thirty-six dollars on her.

"I can take a debit card, if you'd rather not use your cash."

Olivia scowled. "I don't . . . I'll just pay with this." She placed six dollars on the counter.

Janie held a steady gaze on the girl. Seventeen, maybe. Defiant, but scared. Came to Luna on purpose, though unwilling to say why. And had all of thirty-six dollars on her, without a debit card.

What was this girl thinking?

Covering the money Olivia had laid on the counter, Janie pushed the bills back toward the girl. "Keep it."

"Really?" That spark of hope reentered those blue eyes. "But you said . . ."

"I was checking to see if you had money."

And there was the scowl again. "Well, now you know. I do."

"Not much. Not even enough for a full tank of gas. How do you plan to get back to Texas on that?"

"That's none of your business."

Janie sighed as she pressed her palms on the counter. "Olivia, here's the thing. If you don't have money, and you don't have a place to stay, and you don't have a plan, then you're in trouble."

Olivia flinched. Her lips pressed tight, but not enough to hide the quiver.

"Why don't you tell me why you're in Luna, and I'll see what I can do to help?"

"I came to find someone."

"Who?"

She met Janie's stare, her eyes full of fear. "You."

What? "Me? You didn't even know who I was when you walked in."

"You're Janie Truitt, right?"

"Yes . . ."

"Mike Truitt—that's your dad, right?"

Janie's heart stalled, and suddenly the chill from the winter snow settled right there in her café. "How did you know that?"

Olivia ducked. Swallowed. Gripped her mug with both hands. Then looked back up at Janie. "My name is Olivia Truitt."

Janie's head spun as the implication whistled in her brain.

"Mike is my dad too."

And with that bomb, Janie's world became all blur and spin.

A sister.

She had a sister. And, apparently, her dad was still alive.

CHAPTER TWO

"ARE YOU OKAY?"

Bennett looked up from his laptop, his mind still mostly focused on understanding the data that Staci had sent. He looked up at Gemma, who sat curled up in the corner chair near the fire, blanket snug around her legs and a book in hand.

Had his little sister been talking to him? Bennett sifted through the past half an hour since supper, trying to decipher a voice in the background of his concentration. He didn't find one. "Did I miss something?"

Gemma shook her head. "No. I only asked if you were okay."

"Oh." Okay? Why would she ask that? He hadn't been coughing or sniffling, and it'd been over a week since he'd slammed his finger with a hammer while hanging up a picture in her room.

"Are you?" Gemma pressed.

"Sure. Why wouldn't I be?" Bennett leaned back against the wooden dining room chair and stretched.

"You've been . . . quiet." One auburn eyebrow arched over her copper eyes.

Bennett chuckled, hoping the sting of his growing melancholy didn't peep through the mask of his amusement. "Everyone is quiet compared to you, Gem."

Gemma rolled her eyes. "Ha-ha." Laying her book on the arm of her chair, she leaned forward. "I'm serious, Bennett. You've been different. And we don't go up to Hazel's as much as we used to. These days it seems we only go because Nathan decided he wanted to learn how to shoot."

The ball of discomfort rolling in his gut had several layers. One, he had taken Nathan to Hazel to learn how to handle a firearm, and he still wasn't sure how he felt about that. Moving to Montana hadn't yet pried free Bennett's aversion to guns. He had his reasons. And two—the bulk of his angst—Gemma was way too keen in her observations.

Not counting the last time he'd used Nathan as an excuse to go to Elk Lake, he'd not been up to the cabin in fifteen days. Fifteen agonizing, soul-searching, and God-seeking days. And Hazel had only come down to Luna three times in that space.

That made four encounters this month. Four tension-filled meetings in which he felt the full impact of disappointment and hopelessness pressing hard against the love they shared.

And everything before that? Stilted. Every touch stiff. He couldn't get past her proposition before Christmas, and she wasn't yielding on her distrust of marriage. That left them with nearly four months of a tension-filled relationship about which neither wanted to admit the truth.

How could they make it if their beliefs were so different? They were at a dead end.

Bennett had felt certain that God had brought Hazel into his life on purpose, and truly he still believed that was the case. If not for her, for his misadventure at Elk Lake, he'd not have seen his need to change. To repent and to return to the faith and love for God that he'd once had.

But perhaps he'd misunderstood when Hazel had shown up on the Chicago sidewalk that cold winter evening, that orange stocking cap flagging his eye. Perhaps he shouldn't have trusted the hard tug of his heart to hers as she'd swiped away a tear.

Certainly he shouldn't have given in to the passion of his flesh that night when they'd first shared a bed.

There was no undoing any of that.

And there was not a clear direction to go now. Because the thing was, that first night when he'd taken her to his bed, he'd made a silent promise: she'd be his wife. That had been his justification. To himself and to God. He'd sworn in his heart and his mind that he'd marry her.

That seemed to Bennett a binding promise. Even if Hazel hadn't committed to it.

Now it was her, and her alone, in his heart forever, no matter what she did or wouldn't do.

And the other thing was, he loved her. Deeply. Sometimes unreasonably. And at all times completely. Even now, when she'd taken the whole heart he'd held out to her and offered only a fraction of hers in return.

I'll be with you for as long as it suits me. Did she know that was what her suggestion had said to him?

Bennett doubted Hazel understood that, but even with his belief in her ignorance, it hurt.

He loved her though. Even if right now that love was seasoned strongly with ache.

"Bennett?"

Startled, Bennett shook himself, forcing his gaze to focus on Gemma. What has he been staring at? The layers of mountains just beyond the window, dressed in the clean white of crisp snow. The hills that Hazel loved—perhaps more than anything.

Maybe she could see You in them, God? I remember reading in your Word that Your creation declares Your glory . . .

That, more than anything—even more than Hazel loving Bennett—had become his central and greatest hope.

Hazel desperately needed God's salvation and love. Because clearly her and Hunter's reconciliation, while a good thing, was not enough. And the romance between Bennett and Hazel, while a beautiful thing, was not enough.

Hazel needed Jesus.

"See, this is what I'm talking about." Gemma's brow knit. "You're not okay."

Bennett rubbed the back of his head. Thick waves long enough to grip in fistfuls met his hand. Might be time for a haircut. "I'm fine. Don't worry about me, kid."

No, he wasn't fine. He was entirely in love with a woman who desperately needed salvation. That seemed like a hard place to land.

"You and Hazel had a fight. Everything's been all wrong since . . . since Christmas."

Closing his laptop, Bennett pushed the chair back. A fight wasn't quite accurate. They'd reached an impasse, and from where Bennett was, it looked like no matter which way he turned, there was going to be heartache.

"Did you break up?"

"No, Gem." He stood. Swallowed against the squeezing in his chest. He'd considered it—breaking up. Honestly, the question of doing so still weighed in his mind and peppered his prayers. His and Hazel's relationship had been a roller coaster. Long term, that seemed like an unhealthy start. Shouldn't they find something solid to build on? If he said they needed to step back and try for it, could they even manage a friendship now? Would Hazel be willing to try?

Bennett thought of Hunter and Janie—a sharp jab of jealousy poking his heart. For a while, Janie had offered Hunter friendship, and Hunter said he couldn't do it. Not well. And maybe that had more to do with the torture of watching the woman he loved date another man than it did with actually being able to be a friend to that woman. Bennett wasn't sure. But he did know that Hunter had been a knotted mess of volatile emotions throughout that season.

Did Bennett have the sort of character and fortitude to do friendship well with Hazel if they stepped back from the fire of romance?

Doubt seeped like a chilled draft. In his flesh, on his own strength, Bennett was certain the answer was no. Not when what he wanted with every scrap of his will was for Hazel to be his wife. His partner, his lover, his comfort and support and solace and joy. *Just friends* seemed like a paltry alternative to that glorious bond.

"Bennett, you keep staring toward Hazel's mountain like you're homesick." Gemma tossed her blanket to the side and planted her feet on the ground. "Let's just go see her already."

His heart rate spiked. Energy pulsed through his veins as though he was standing at the start of a race, not in the middle of his living room. And yet caution tugged him back.

What would he say to Hazel? *I missed you. Needed to see you, to hear you say that you love me. To tell you, yet again, that I love you and want a life with you . . .*

He'd said it all before. Every time he'd walked away with another nick in his heart.

I think we need to step back. Try being friends.

He wouldn't get through those two sentences without weeping. Just the thought of them made his eyes burn.

"Bennett?" Gemma stood, hands popped on her hips. She nodded, as if the decision was made. "I'll get Nathan. And then when we're at the cabin, we'll wander over to see the lodge. Maybe Hunter will have something we can help him with."

Bennett didn't respond, and Gemma took his silence as a yes. She scampered up the stairs, yelling for Nathan as she went.

He wanted to go. Needed to see Hazel. Then again, he wasn't sure he could face her. Not when his mind had nearly accepted the course his heart didn't want to take.

He'd table that decision. For just a little longer. Then?

What was he to do—say—when he faced Hazel?

The tack room.

He'd ordered a new latch. It had come in last week. It'd be a chore to replace the simple, old sliding closer—the one that locked the door from the outside. The job was on the more high-level side of Bennett's skills. But he had wanted that latch replaced since the day he'd accidentally locked Hazel in the tack room.

It was the perfect excuse. They could be there together and say nothing about the tension that stretched between them.

And maybe she'd see that the last thing in the world Bennett wanted was for her to feel trapped.

CHAPTER THREE

HAZEL LOOKED UP FROM the words she'd been reading—and rereading several times over—and scanned the vista at her feet. A blanket of white disguised much of the black earth that led to the drop, but she knew the path enough. Strange how the past few weeks she'd been drawn back up to this spot, when most of her life she'd avoided it. In fact, in the past decade, she'd only come to Black Gulch that one time with Bennett last summer.

Her third visit in a month.

She couldn't explain that. It wasn't as though she wanted to be there. Not as if she had some morbid sense of connection to the place where her parents had died and the area where they'd spread their ashes—and that of her grandparents.

But the loneliness that carved within felt something like that severe gouge in the mountain. Deep and black and terrifying.

And since she'd pulled the book from Nan's small collection of literature, Hazel had found herself braving the steep trail to the gulch. Not for connection. Some unknowable draw brought her. There, tucked into a protected crevasse of stone, facing south where the sun could warm her cold toes, she'd sat for several hours and read. As she had done on her other two unaccounted visits.

And as she did so, the tumultuous void within continued to roil with a demand to be filled.

Hazel pushed against that silent observation, determined to ignore the unruly discontentment. Instead, she focused on what she loved—the whisper of wind through the trees, the bold rise of the ancient mountains, and the knowledge that all this could not be stripped away.

Her sole stability in life.

The Black Gulch seemed to mock her attempt at self-comfort. One bad decision, one wrongly placed step, and the granite could take away the very breath of life.

At least, from this tucked away spot, she couldn't see the actual gulch. She could see the plane of the ledge but not the heart-stopping face of the vertical drop. If she didn't know it was there, in fact, she wouldn't have guessed.

The view here was particularly stunning.

Past the cliff's edge and the span of the gorge that wasn't quite visible from this angle, the rise of the next layered peak climbed with commanding authority. It met the sky with white-capped glory on that day, gleaming with glittery iridescence in the unfiltered sunlight. The wide expanse of deep-blue sky made the perfect backdrop.

Her mom had called that rise the Gulch Prince. Hazel had no idea if that was what was labeled on a survey map, but it was what she knew it as.

The Gulch Prince watched my parents die.

She'd thought the very thing when she'd glimpsed that regal peak as a girl. Tears had burned against the rims of her eyes, and her throat had swelled with the need to cry. But as her heart had hardened with resentment toward that merciless, silent monarch of stone, young Hazel had glanced at Pops.

Pops hadn't cried. He'd glared at the gulch that had claimed the life of his only child. And then rolled his hands tight. "Zach should have known better."

Zach . . . Zachary Edmond Wallace. Her father. The one who had been born to these hills, a man who'd climbed rocks because cheating death was an addiction.

"Letti knew what she was doing too," Nan had said softly. "It was a freak storm. No one could have predicted—"

Letti, Hazel's mother. A woman *not* born to Elk Lake Canyon but whose adventurous spirit had claimed it as her own. The very spirit that Zachary had fallen in love with. They were determined to live life free and daring. Their motto: never let a day pass without a thrill.

Pops had aimed a harsh glare on Nan, shook his head, and strode back down the trail the way they'd come up. He was never the same again.

Hazel found she was staring at the sight of that memory—the place where they'd spread her parents' ashes. Her eyelids burned—those tears still not yet allowed their freedom. She shifted her attention back to the Gulch Prince.

"You watched them die . . ." she whispered, the words harsh. And perhaps not at all aimed at the mountain.

A tear rolled against her nose.

She lifted her gaze higher, above the shimmering white crown of that mountain and into the azure depths beyond. "You let them die."

Hazel clutched the book in her hand, pressing it into her chest. She had known the adventurous tales of Mr. Lewis in his wardrobe books, but never had she delved into Nana's small collection of his nonfiction works.

Right then she wished she hadn't allowed her curiosity to rule her reading choices. Because now she not only had the dizzying and heart-wrenching problem of what to do with Bennett Crofton—the man she loved and needed and didn't want to lose and yet couldn't give a promise of forever to—but she must come back to this place, the moment, and face the pain that had triggered a silent, cold war between her and . . .

"What are you doing here?"

Hunter's deep voice stirred Hazel from her spiraling thoughts. She whipped around, peeking past the boulder that had sheltered her from the northern breeze, and watched her brother climb the remaining distance to her spot.

She swallowed as he lowered himself beside her. "Are you following me?"

"Yeah, actually." He looked at her with curiosity. "I was out checking the game trails, and I saw you veer off the trap line. This isn't one of your typical treks."

Hazel squared her shoulders. "How would you know?"

He didn't blink. "I know you, little sis." For a long moment, he simply held her in his stare. Like he was searching for something. Then he whispered, "What brings you to the Black Gulch?"

She sighed, leaning heavily into the rock at her back. "Questions, I guess."

"Are you finding answers?"

"No." The word came out harsh.

Hunter tapped the volume in her hands. "Good book?"

"Not really."

He turned the spine so he could read the title. "C. S. Lewis? How could that not be good?"

"The stories in here aren't like his lion books. They're . . . they're of his life. What he thought and believed."

"Ah. He was a Christian."

"Not always."

"And you hoped he'd help you find answers?"

"No." Hazel tucked the book beside her hip, out of his reach. "I found this with some of Nan's things. I remembered her reading it, so I wanted to see what was there. Mostly, it's confusing. And sad sometimes."

Hunter nodded. "His mother died when he was a boy, right?"

She clenched her jaw and nodded. That wasn't all that had been sad in his life. But she wasn't going to make a list.

Hunter propped up an elbow on his knee and stared out at the Gulch Prince. For several moments they sat in silence, which should have felt normal. Instead, the chasm within moaned and writhed yet again.

Hazel couldn't shush it. "If there is a god, how could he let such things happen?"

Beside her, Hunter stirred. She refused to look at him, keeping her glare on the Prince. When his arm settled on her shoulders, she sucked in a startled breath. "That's a big, complicated question," he said. "One that implies that you're mad at God."

God.

"I don't even know if I believe in God."

"Hmm."

She squinted up at him, not appreciating that doubtful tone.

"Hazel, I think you know there's a God. And maybe you're mad at Him. But I don't think that's really what is bothering you now. Why you come up here, when the Black Gulch scares you."

"What does that mean?"

"I think you feel a deep emptiness—bigger and more terrifying than the gulch. I think you feel like if you can stare down your fear of this place, you'll fill in what you don't understand in here." He tapped her chest.

"That's presumptuous of you."

He shook his head. "No. I've been on this trail, and I know the fight." He leaned back, withdrawing his arm. "The thing is, you're not going to silence the ache. You're not going to be able to fill the void. Not with Elk Lake, or by facing this gulch, or even with Bennett Crofton."

She scowled at him. "I don't think I want to hear this."

"Hear what?"

"That I'm broken and there isn't any hope."

As Hunter tipped his head to the side, his expression softened. "I know, Zel. But there are things we all must hear. Must face. One of them is that we're broken—but there is hope."

She shook her head and moved to stand, but Hunter stalled her escape with a hand on her elbow. "Hazel, you *need* to hear this. God is real. And He cares. And it is His love that will give life and peace to your soul. He's the only one who will fill that void you don't want to admit you have."

Hazel pulled her arm from his grasp but found that she couldn't charge away. Instead, she looked toward that mocking Prince, fighting for control over the surge of emotion Hunter had provoked.

She wasn't broken. *Then why can't you commit to Bennett? Why are all of your relationships so hard?*

She didn't need help. *Then why do you tremble at this ache?*

She didn't believe in God. *Then why do Hunter's words upset you so much?*

She cleared her throat and glared back at her brother. "Why is this so important to you?"

"Because I love you." Hunter let that simple, profound declaration lay on its own. After a beat, he leaned forward and brushed Hazel's nose with a fingertip, then stood to leave. He took a step and then looked down at her. "You've always fought against it. The thing is, Hazel, at some point, if you're not careful, you'll get your way. You'll be left alone. I love you too much to not say something before that happens."

Then he walked back down the trail, his steps a firm crunch on the dirt and stone.

Hazel felt his retreat deeply. All the way into that void she couldn't ignore. What had he meant—she fought against what?

Love? God? Both?

Haze was a simple girl. She liked life straightforward. Uncomplicated.

If she didn't want to feel the overwhelming, lung-crushing grief of her parents' death, she didn't visit the Black Gulch. That had worked for so long. But there she sat. Remembering. Writhing.

If she didn't want to deal with the conflict of someone else's will coming up against her own, she ignored that other person until they left her alone to have her way.

That had worked for so long. But she didn't want to be left alone. Not by Hunter and certainly not by Bennett.

If she didn't want to wrestle with the contradiction of knowing there was a God who had made the mountains she loved, and also knowing that same God had allowed her young heart to get shredded, she simply denied believing He was there all together.

That had worked for so long.

Now it wasn't working. None of that was working. And she was afraid that Hunter might be right—she was getting her way. Only, she didn't really want it.

Moose stood from his dry spot under the front deck, let out one welcoming bark, and wagged his tail. Bennett grinned, the delight in being welcomed as one who belonged a comfort. No matter what tensions pulled between him and Hazel, Moose never wavered in his loyalty. To both of them.

That took a special kind of love. Perhaps one that only dogs possessed.

Nathan and Gemma exited the vehicle, called a quick "see ya," and raced each other to the ridge trail—Nathan with a fading limp on his air-cast leg. Bennett wasn't sure what had earned Hunter favorite status with both kids, but it didn't matter. He was glad they were excited for something in this whirlwind life they'd been tossed into. And glad it was Hunter.

He was a good man. Working hard to be a godly man. Bennett couldn't ask for better for his younger siblings in the way of a role model, and he was grateful.

Shutting the driver's-side door to his Jeep, Bennett scanned Elk Lake. Cold days and even colder nights had frozen the surface solid, and a fresh blanket of white made it look like an expanse of treeless meadow. Only the dock, which still held the twin Adirondack chairs he'd purchased last spring, signaled that water was beneath the clean white spread.

Moose lumbered to Bennett's side and slid his head under Bennett's palm. "Hey, boy. Is she here?"

Tail wagging, Moose simply panted his delight and waited for Bennett to decide where to go.

A series of well-packed trails cut from the cabin, each toward a specific destination. One to the shack, which would likely sit empty for the next several weeks, as Hazel and Hunter didn't have any clients on schedule. From that trail, another branched off toward the dock.

Hazel spent every evening on that old wood extension, to watch the sunset, if not to fish. Bennett had no problem envisioning her at the end of the dock, savoring the glory of the evening sky.

If he had his way, he'd be right there with her. Every night, her filling his arms while wonder brimmed full in his heart.

A twinge of frustration clenched in his chest. Bennett moved his study toward the other trails.

Around the opposite way from the shack and the dock, a path wound toward the rise west of the cabin. At the place where the slope lifted sharply, that path also cut into two. One went up—toward old the Wallace trapline that ran parallel to the upper creek. The other, over the ridge toward the lodge.

Bennett studied those trails, wondering which of them Hazel was most likely on—because he felt certain she wasn't in the cabin. Not only was that not something Hazel did much—hanging around indoors—but the three missing dogs were the sure sign. Anyway, if she were there, she would have heard his vehicle.

"Hazel?" Bennett stepped onto the path that unified all the others—the one that would take him to the front of the cabin. Moose stayed at his heels, and they both wandered to the side of the deck where the stairs were. "Where did she head off to today, bud?"

Moose turned, and his long legs took him around the back side of the cabin. Toward the corral and tack room. Bennett followed.

Everything was neat and quiet. Mule and Pony stood at the feed bunk, noses buried in the pile of clean hay. No Mr. Big though.

Bennett rubbed Moose's head. "She went for a ride, hmm?"

Moose sat looking up at him, as though proud.

Bennett chuckled. "Look at me and you. Not so long ago, you terrified me."

That long pink tongue lolled to the side, and when Bennett scratched Moose's head, the bearlike dog shut his eyes and smiled.

Hazel was right. Dogs smiled. They talked. You just had to learn their language—and be one of the few who were allowed into their world. He was honored to be such a one.

Bennett had learned so much over the past year. Changed so much. Everything felt different and new—and that was a good thing. Standing there in the snow, at the site where God had reopened his eyes, offered him a chance to start anew, and the wonder of mercy washed over him yet again.

He hadn't deserved such grace. But God had offered it. Freely. Abundantly. Wondrously.

As emotion churned in his soul, Bennett buried his hand in the thick fur of his companion, lifted his face toward the sky, and squeezed his eyes shut. "Do it again, Lord." A sting of warmth lined his eyelids as he prayed. Begged. "Please, Father, I know You love her. Even more than I do."

Hazel had changed over the months too. But she still needed Jesus. She didn't know it, but Bennett knew she felt it. She wouldn't be so afraid if she didn't. And she wouldn't be searching . . .

Once again the tension of loving the fierce little mountain lioness God had used to change his life, and not knowing what to do with their relationship, strained his heart. A small window of clarity had cracked in his understanding, but that didn't make it easier. Mostly because it wasn't what he wanted. But also, because he wasn't sure how to implement the shift.

How did he convince the woman he loved—the one to whom he'd proposed marriage—that stepping back, working on a solid friendship, wasn't the same thing as breaking up?

He felt like Jacob, wrestling with God as he begged for strength to face what must be done and blessing in whatever happened after.

Bennett released anxiety from his lungs. One day at a time, he supposed. There were things he could do as he went—practical things. That slide latch on the tack room, for example. "I've got something for that."

With a shot of a grin toward Moose, he walked back to his car. Once there he gathered the supplies—the new lock as well as the battery-powered drill, the bits, and the extra hardware he'd tossed into a box—most of which came from the old hardware store Mom had recently acquired.

A God-working, as Mama B had called it. Tellings Hardware had been boarded up and untouched for the last forty years, ever since Jed Tellings had dropped dead of a heart attack. His kids, all three of whom had long since left Luna, hadn't been able to agree on what to do with the place.

It was a historic cornerstone of Luna—one of the first businesses to open in the old mountain town—so it should remain. But no one wanted to run it. And no one wanted to hire out someone who would. So they should sell it. But that hadn't been acceptable to the oldest son.

So it had sat. For decades. Closed up, useless, and untouched. Until the day after Thanksgiving.

Mom had asked real estate agent Leslie Yates about the building. Located next to the Pantry, it would make an ideal location for her clinic—should a doctor out of Big Sky agree to be Mom's cooperating provider, and that was looking promising.

But the building hadn't been for sale.

Leslie had made the call anyway—and it seemed to be perfect timing. The three siblings had grudgingly come together for the holiday, and the gathering had been all spite and tension. Which was sad. But also had pried the door open for negotiation. Seemed after forty years of bickering about the old store, all three were ready to wash their hands of it.

Sell? If the price was right.

Good thing Mom had owned a house in a nice Chicago suburb. And as a woman, she had access to some substantial business subsidies. Not to mention the grants available for remote medical service providers. She was confident she'd make the financials work.

It was all falling into place. Like a God-working.

Bennett chuckled at Mama B's wording and lifted a silent praise. These little things—or maybe not so small—helped soothe his worried heart. And they reminded him that he had a much-too-small view of God.

Having carried his tools to the corral, Bennett stopped at the gate and hesitated before he opened it. Lifting his face to the warmth of the golden sun, which felt like a glorious contradiction to the chill of the December day, he exhaled.

"There is no one like You, God. You are no ordinary Savior. Not a man who can only do limited things. You are the God of the universe. You rule over the night and the day. You sit enthroned in glory. There is nothing too hard for You. No heart that is too far gone.

"You called me out of a life of dark selfishness. Took this man who lived only for pleasure and gain and replaced his heart of stone.

"Nothing is impossible with You."

Hope and peace reclaimed the frazzled corners of Bennett's soul. He opened the gate, strode to the tack room, and got to work.

CHAPTER FOUR

HUNTER COULD HEAR GEMMA laughing before either sibling emerged from the snow-dusted pines at the back of the lodge. Her infectious joy—oftentimes faked—made him grin. More and more, as the weeks had worn on, it seemed her facade of *everything is fine* was fading and something real—and surprisingly still happy—was replacing the mask.

Gemma was a special kid. She'd landed in all their hearts—his and Janie's. Bennett's. Hazel's. Mama B's. Even Bennett's mom's, Tara. Gemma's determination to make the best out of life, even if it seemed like a crapshoot, was nothing short of admirable. And it seemed to be wearing off on Nathan—despite his efforts to defy it.

Hunter wandered from the front deck of the lodge—cup of coffee steaming in the cold mountain air. As he passed by one of the four giant windows facing the pond, he glanced inside. The contractor laying the tile in the large kitchen at the back of the lodge poked his head through the wide passage that would eventually hold double swinging doors. Grout tool in hand, the man spoke with Evan, Hunter's general contractor.

There didn't seem to be a sign of an issue between them, so Hunter trusted there wasn't one and continued to stride across the finished deck until he came to the side steps. There he watched and waited while Gemma's voice rang through the thin, crisp air.

"No excuses, Nathan. If I win, it's fair and square."

"I'm still limping!"

"But not too much!" She giggled and then squealed. "That's cheating, Nate!"

A quieter, lower chuckle sounded from the nearby trees. "A little snow never hurt anyone."

Hunter laughed. His guess—Nathan had just nailed Gemma with a snowball. Something Hunter would have done to Hazel. By the sound of Gemma's reaction, she was less angry than determined.

They were good for each other, those two. Even if they were completely different. Again, like Hunter and Hazel.

Nathan had become more . . . *not* awful. He improved particularly whenever someone invested in teaching him how to become a man, rather than brushing him off as a nuisance kid. Like when Hunter asked him to build a fire or help him chop wood. Or when Hazel taught him how to shoot a rifle and took him out for target practice. Even Bennett had warmed to the tactic, asking Nathan to help with the harder tasks, like shoveling snow or building the wall-length bookshelves that Bennett had put in under the stairs at his Victorian house.

Seemed every time Nathan felt he could be a useful human—and a man at that—his need to be a punk shrank. Hunter—if not all of them—could only hope and pray that would continue. Because the kid still needed a chip-ectomy from his shoulder when it came to things like not being a jerk to his sister. Or to Bennett's mom.

Patience. And hope. That was what they all needed.

Gemma burst from the tree line, hair dusted with white powder, cheeks rosy, and a determined smirk on her face. She ran straight for the woodpile, slid around the back side of it, and ducked behind the four feet of split logs.

Leaning against the bulky wood post that supported the cover for the deck, Hunter crossed his arms and waited to see if Nathan would figure out his sister's ploy.

A flash of black—likely Nathan's coat—glinted around the trees at the trail's mouth. But then it retreated. Hunter followed the blip of the boy's silhouette as he wove between trees, working his way around the woodpile.

Clever boy.

Suddenly he stepped from the shelter of the trees, now behind Gemma's hiding spot near the frozen edge of the pond. Both fists loaded with a freshly made snowball, Nathan crept nearer. A good trick for him to accomplish, as he did still limp. Then he stood straight and fired.

"Hey!" Gemma yelped and then leapt from her hiding spot. She laughed, though she ran straight for her brother. "That was sneaky!"

Nathan also laughed as he fired his second ball. This time he missed, and Gemma didn't slow down. She barreled into her older brother, and both tumbled into the snow.

"Better call a truce." Hunter stepped off the deck, smiling. "Before you're both too cold and wet and Nathan injures that leg again."

Gemma rolled off her brother and onto her back, her shoulders shaking with laughter. "You didn't think I could take you down, did you?"

Nathan looked like a happy little boy as he shot a grin toward her.

Hunter's heart danced. This was not a scene he would have imagined witnessing between these two a few months back.

So much had changed. For all of them.

Thank You, God, for that.

"Come on, both of you." He lifted his mug and tossed his head toward the lodge. "I've got hot chocolate waiting for you, and Janie texted to say she'd be up in a little while."

"Woo-hoo!" Gemma scrambled to her feet and did a little happy dance. "I didn't know Janie was coming! We can look at her wedding dress again."

Hunter wanted to shout his own hallelujah at the mention of the wedding. His wedding. The one when he'd finally, at long-stink-ing-forever-last marry the girl who had owned his whole heart since he'd been fifteen years old. Finally, Janie would be his wife. Forever and ever, amen.

Thank You, God, for that!

Not even trying to tame his smile at such a giddy thought, Hunter led the way to his trailer. Ahem. His *trash can*, as both Hazel and Janie insisted. Eh. What could you do? No use arguing with two stubborn women when they've got their minds stuck on a thing. Anyway, it didn't matter. Once the lodge was done—a day nearing as quickly as the wedding—the trailer would be gone. Just a memory of a time that was a struggle ... but had brought him to something amazing.

To the Splendor.

His grin eased, but not because his heart felt any less joy. Now, it was just more awesome wonder than giddy joy. When he'd settled on the name for his lodge, it wasn't just because of the view—though the glorious vista did figure into it. He'd named the lodge Lake Shore Splendor because it was there, on those redemption shores, that he'd first witnessed and understood the splendor of God—the God who granted mercy and grace. Who held out salvation to a wretched man like Hunter.

He'd named it the Splendor so he would never forget. Never make God's love less. With all of his heart, he wanted to always remember the wonder of it.

At the trailer, he popped open the narrow door and ducked in-side.

Holding the aluminum doorframe, Gemma peeked in behind him but didn't climb through—likely because there wasn't room. "When are you going to move out of this thing?"

Hunter gathered two insulated metal mugs, two hot chocolate packets, and the electric teakettle that still held hot water. "As soon as the carriage house passes inspection."

"How long will that be?" This came from Nathan, who stood back from the trailer, near Hunter's outdoor fire ring.

"Hopefully, before the wedding."

Gemma took the hot teakettle. "Oh! We should have a party!"

"You always want to have a party, Gem." Nathan rolled his eyes.

Hunter set both mugs on the overturned stump he used as a side table. "Nathan's not wrong."

Shrugging, Gemma topped the powder mixes Hunter had dumped in the mugs with hot water. "Why not? Celebrate what you can when you can, right?"

"Is that some TikTok challenge or something?"

Gemma made a sassy face. "No, Mr. Wet Blanket. At least, I don't know. Bennett made me get rid of TikTok. And everything else except Insta."

"Why'd he do that?" Hunter asked.

"He said when you try to be everywhere all the time, you lose who you really are. It's better to be your whole best self in one place than be a fragmented fake all over." She shrugged, as if she wasn't sure that was true. "Or maybe he just didn't want to have to keep track of me and all my socials. Narrowing it down to one is a lot easier."

Smart. How'd Bennett know to do that?

"Do you miss it?" Hunter asked.

"TikTok?"

He nodded.

Gemma stirred her hot cocoa. "I thought I would a lot more than I do. But not really. There's a lot to do here IRL, you know?"

"IRL?"

"In real life," Nathan said.

Hunter looked at him. "How about you? I suppose Bennett made you get rid of some things."

Nathan sipped his hot chocolate. "Nope."

"That's because he wasn't on anything." Gemma rolled her eyes, like her brother was the lamest. "He just chats with his gamers, and they have their own space in Discord."

"What is Discord?"

"Gamers' chat space," Nathan answered.

Hunter lowered onto another overturned log. "What's your favorite game?"

"I'm into battle royales right now. *Call of Duty Black Ops 4, Blackout mode* is pretty intense."

"I stopped gaming a while ago—found out I thought about it in my sleep and couldn't concentrate on my job, which doesn't fly in the navy. Tell me what *Blackout* mode is."

Nathan's eyes lit. "Like I said, it's a battle royale format. Kind of like the *Hunger Games*, where you get dropped into this arena. You don't have any weapons or really any idea what you're getting into. And then you have to stay alive. Gather weapons. Stay alive. Keep away from other players. Survive. And the arena shrinks, so you have to keep moving and adapting. It's pretty intense."

This was truly Nathan's jam. Maybe Hunter would have to try gaming again, to engage with Nathan where he thrived. The trick of it being both of them still needed to live in reality. Experience had already informed Hunter on how difficult that could be. If they could agree on good boundaries and stay accountable though . . .

He'd think on it. Talk to Janie to get her take. And Bennett and probably John Brighton.

The sound of snow crunching under tires drew their attention toward the road, hidden behind them.

"Man, that was fast." Gemma gave a rare frown. "I thought they'd talk a lot longer than that."

"Who?"

She looked at Hunter, worry in her expression. "Bennett and Hazel. Something is wrong with them."

It was? Hunter looked at Nathan, who dug his good foot into the snow at the base of his overturned log stool. The boy's brow also furrowed the way Gemma's had. With concern.

"What's going on?"

Nathan shrugged. "They're just off." He shot a warning glare at Gemma. "It's probably nothing. We should have stayed out of it instead of dragging Bennett up here when he didn't want to."

Bennett didn't want to come to the lake? He didn't want to see Hazel? That didn't sound right at all.

Before Hunter could press for more information, the nose of the vehicle came through the wall of evergreens. Janie, not Bennett.

"Oh!" Gemma's bright sunshine returned lickety-split. "False alarm. It's Janie!"

Hunter felt the surge of pleasure, warm and spiked with adrenaline, just like he always did when Janie came his way. But along with that was a cool chill of unease. What was going on with his sister and her boyfriend? How long had there been a problem? And should he intrude on it?

Did Janie know what was going on?

Hunter dug his stocking cap out of his coat pocket and snugged it over his head while the flurry of questions gusted through his mind. He walked toward the car as Janie parked. Gemma and Nathan stayed put by the cold fire ring—Hunter's guess, because Nathan told Gemma to sit and wait a second.

Sometimes the boy could be intuitive. When he paid attention.

Janie slid out of her car, wearing buffalo-checked insulated boots Hunter had given her for Christmas. He grinned as another spike of that warm adrenaline washed through his veins. If giving her the things that she had casually mentioned she liked earned him the sweet kisses she'd given him that day, he'd do it as often as possible, holiday or not. For the rest of his life.

Sweet blue eyes met him as he stepped to her side. "Hi, mountain man."

Leaning down, Hunter caught her upturned lips with his own. One kiss. Maybe two . . . "Hi, sweetie."

Lowering from her toe-lifted height, she laid a hand on his chest and looked past him. "I see you have company."

"I do. They're excited you're here too. Gemma is hoping you've got more bridal magazines. And she wants to see your dress again."

"You haven't peeked at it, right?" She eyed him.

Hands up, he shook his head. "No, ma'am. I want to see you in it coming down those stairs, ready to make me a king."

Janie chuckled and shook her head. "Gemma would have us hold the most ostentatious wedding Luna has ever seen, if I'd let her."

Hunter wrapped her hand in his, a thrill sparking at the feel of that cold metal ring on her fourth finger. He shrugged. "Showy. Plain. I don't care. Just as long as at the end of the thing, you're my wife."

"Maybe we should have eloped."

"I think I suggested that." True statement. It might have been in a moment of impatient passion and said for entirely selfish reasons. But he *had* suggested it.

Janie smirked. "We've been through enough to warrant a day to look back on and remember. Something happy and beautiful that marks the transition, don't you think?"

"I think you deserve whatever you want." He lifted her hand to press her knuckles to his lips. "So in the words of Westley, my love, *as you wish.*"

She nudged him with her shoulder. "I'm sure this romantic side of you isn't going to last forever, but I'll take it for as long as you're going to give it."

"That stings, Janie girl. I'm completely romantic."

"Says the mountain man who lives in a trash-can trailer and who, for our first date, brought trail mix and deer jerky on a hike." Janie wrinkled her nose and shook her head in exaggerated disgust.

Hunter swept the view in front of them with his hand. "Your castle is in the works, my lady. Complete with a gourmet kitchen at your disposal. If I'm not mistaken, that gives you two kitchens to make all the yummy food you want, sans the deer jerky."

Janie looked up at him, love warm in her gaze. But then that emotion shifted to something less warm. Not angry. But . . . maybe worry?

"What's wrong?"

Her lips pressed, and she glanced toward the kids, who were still waiting at the fire ring. Looking back up to Hunter, she raised to press a kiss to his whiskered cheek. "We'll talk about it later. I have wedding planning to do."

Janie took two strides forward, but Hunter tugged her to a stop. "Am I in trouble?"

"No." She smiled. There was that warm love again, though the reserved concern still lingered. "Not today."

He'd have to wait, then. Hunter stifled a sigh. Seemed every season of joy came with touches of difficulty.

Janie dusted happy back on her face and walked toward the Croftons. "Hi, Gem! Ready to pull out some magazines?"

"Yes, ma'am!" Gemma lifted her mug in a *cheers* gesture. "I've been watching reruns of *Say Yes to the Dress*. I'm certain we picked exactly the right neckline for you!"

Hunter snorted. Janie would look divine in a burlap bag, necklines being irrelevant. His gaze tracked the two girls as they nearly skipped to the lodge. Gemma snagged Janie's hand and led her onward.

The wedding mattered to Janie—Hunter knew it did. But not just for herself and not just for them as a couple. This planning and excitement was something she could give Gemma, and that made Janie happy.

Hunter fell a little deeper in love with the woman's beautiful heart.

"Didn't you tell me never to fall in love?" Nathan's mild snark drew Hunter's stare from the girls just as they rounded out of sight onto the front deck.

"What?"

"Yep. I remember it clearly. You said, 'Never fall in love. You'll never think straight again.'" Nathan raised an amused brow.

"I was half-right. The part about thinking straight." He stepped behind Nathan and squeezed his shoulder. "But thinking straight might be overrated. You should definitely fall in love someday. With a good woman."

"And here I thought you were a tough mountain man."

Hunter rounded Nathan to face him, playfully putting up his fists and working a cross jab into an uppercut. "You finish your rehab, kid, and I'll show you a thing or two."

"You gonna fight me?"

Lowering his fists, Hunter rolled his eyes and mussed Nathan's knitted beanie, which covered his shaggy dark hair. "No, dude. That'd be dumb. I'll teach you to box though. If you want."

"Yeah?"

Hunter held out a fist. "Yeah."

Nathan bumped it, then fell into step beside Hunter. "Think Bennett will go for that?"

Hunter glanced toward the ridge trail, as if the man in question would stroll into view. They should talk—he and Bennett. Seemed like the man had made himself scarce over the past few weeks. Or Hunter had been so swept up in the elation of finally having Janie back in his arms that he forgot about being a friend.

Hadn't even gone to Bible study in several weeks. That wasn't good.

Hunter turned back to Nathan. "I think so." He swept his hand toward the lodge. "Let's go catch up with the girls before they can plan a party larger than this lodge can hold."

Nathan's right brow arched. "Have you met my sister?"

"We'd better get in there."

CHAPTER FIVE

MR. BIG MOSEYED AROUND the stand of aspens as he wandered the familiar path back to the cabin. Hazel had let him find his own way back as she rode relaxed, her mind not on the trail but consumed with what she'd recently read from Lewis.

God cannot give us a happiness and peace apart from Himself, because it is not there. There is no such thing.

She didn't understand Mr. Lewis's writings. But she couldn't stop reading them. Or pondering his words.

What did he mean, there was no such thing as happiness apart from God? Seemed like people of all sorts were happy at some point or another.

She'd been happy. Hadn't she? Alone. Safe at her lake . . . She'd been fine.

Why was she not fine now? Why did she have this driving thirst for . . . for something. She had more now than she did back when she was happy on her own. Specifically, she had Bennett.

Bennett made her happy.

Didn't he?

Ugh. This spiraling, dizzying turn of thoughts. She should stop reading *Mere Christianity*. It wasn't helping—and Hazel hadn't been looking for help in the first place. She'd just wondered why Nan had kept that book separate from all the others. Why it had been tucked securely in the nightstand on Nan's side of the bed. Why there had been so many pages dogeared.

She should put it back where she found it. Go back to ignoring the little hardback edition.

But she couldn't go back. Not to being happy alone on her lake. Not to not having read Mr. Lewis's confusing words.

She had unknowingly plunged herself into a realm of unsatisfied thirst and knotted up, confusing emotion. And all she could think was *make it stop*.

Make it stop so she go back to being happy. Make it stop so she could live in peace. Make it stop so she didn't feel lost anymore.

How could she make it stop?

The conversation with her brother hadn't helped. If anything, Hunter had made it worse.

Mr. Big stepped into the small clearing, and the cabin came into view. Off to the side and a bit behind that was the corral. Pony and Mule stood at attention, their interest fixed on the tack room shed.

On the man at the door of the tack room shed.

Heart clenching, Hazel sucked in a breath. How could seeing him electrify her even now? They'd been together a year, and the sight of Bennett still snatched her breath and made her antsy.

Perhaps it did now since they'd not been in sync the past few weeks. Or months. She'd barely seen him, and when she had, it'd been strained. The echoes of her asking him to move in last Thanksgiving had become faint strains of flat notes in the back of her mind. And the sad, slow shake of his head, along with the dullness of his gaze as he'd whispered "It's been a good day. Let's not ruin it" replayed slowly against the disappointment of her heart. The light in his eyes had failed to return. At least, not fully.

And so there they were, stuck in the tension of an endless loop of that ill-begotten moment. Forever?

Please, God, no.

In the back, cluttered corner of her mind, Hazel wondered if that thought was a prayer or merely a reaction. Whatever it was, she'd been doing it a lot lately. Ever since Nathan had wandered off and gotten himself hurt last fall.

You do believe in God.

That panicked shot toward heaven *had* been prayer. The certainty of it stirred discomfort in her mind. What did it mean that when crisis hit, she suddenly prayed?

The man at the tack room straightened and turned, likely alerted to her approach by Moose, who had been lying in the sun near the corral fence, until he woke up and stood, panting at the sight of Hazel and Mr. Big.

Bennett straightened from whatever it was he was doing to the door and lifted a hand. "Hi there, stranger."

His easygoing greeting soothed a good bit of her nerves.

Hazel tugged on the reins and didn't wait for Mr. Big to come to a complete stop before she slid from the saddle. Shading her eyes from the bright winter sun, she snatched up the reins and walked the rest of the space to the fence where Bennett waited. "Surprise," she said.

He looped an arm over the fence separating them. "A good one, I hope."

She smiled, then raised up on her booted toes and pressed a kiss into his groomed beard. "Always."

Her heart stammered. It'd been near to three weeks since she'd *really* kissed this man. How had that happened? He'd moved to Luna so they would be closer, but since his relocation, she'd felt his heart retreating.

Bennett reached across the fence and cupped her cheek in his cold, rough hand. His thumb brushed across her cheekbone. "I'm glad to hear that."

Once again on her toes, Hazel moved to touch her mouth to his. Hesitancy marked his returned kiss. She sighed as she lowered away. "What are you doing?" She gestured toward the tack room.

With a *come on* wave, Bennett pushed away from the fence, took the three steps required so he could open the gate, and waited for her to pass through. Hazel slid the headstall from Mr. Big's ears and removed the bit, then followed Bennett to the tack room.

He motioned toward the door. "Ta-da!"

A new latch. One that had a lift rather than a slide. Bennett raised the metal closer, opened the door wide, and pointed to the inside of the system. It looked exactly the same, which meant she could open the door from the inside too.

No more getting locked in.

Gratitude filled her heart as she raised her gaze to meet those blue eyes. "You fixed it."

He nodded. "I don't ever want you to feel trapped again. Not if I can help it."

There was weight to that—more meaning than a door and a tack room and a miserable memory of a night spent locked inside. Hazel bit her bottom lip, moving her attention back to the door because she wasn't sure what to do with the intense emotion in Bennett's eyes.

She looked to the ground next. Then fiddled with the leather straps in her hand.

Bennett stepped back. "I thought you'd be happy."

"I am." She was. But why did she feel like crying too? "Thank you. It was thoughtful of you."

Bennett held his gaze on her for two more heartbeats and then turned to walk toward Mr. Big. Without another word, he worked on the cinch buckle, let it loose, and pulled the saddle off, blanket and all. Still quiet, he took saddle and blanket to the tack room, settled the saddle on the tree, and draped the padded blanket over the leather seat, just as she'd shown him before.

Hazel followed, hanging the headstall and reins on a peg.

"Hazel."

"Bennett."

Their anxious voices sounded at the same time. Bennett gestured toward her. "Go ahead."

Hazel shoved her hands into her coat pocket. "I was just going to say that maybe we should talk."

"Yeah." Bennett nodded. "Me too. We haven't . . . not really. Not since . . ."

"Thanksgiving." How had it been that long? Months—*months!*—had gone by with the pair of them in this terrible shadow.

She swallowed. "Maybe . . . do you want to come in?" Hands stuffed in her coat pockets, she motioned with her elbow toward the cabin. "I can make you something warm to drink."

"Sure." Bennett rubbed the back of his neck. "That sounds good. Let me pick up here, and I'll meet you inside."

"Okay." Hazel walked back out into the sun. She stopped at the open door and tried the new latch. The metal clinked as she raised and lowered the mechanism on the inside. "This is . . ." She looked back at Bennett, who had followed her back outside. "This is perfect, Benji. Thank you."

Those beautiful blue eyes held layers of stormy emotion. Ache. Longing. Regret. Love. A ghost of a smile lifted one corner of his mouth, then he bent and brushed a gentle kiss against her cheek. "You're welcome."

Oh, but she wanted only the love.

Once in the cabin, Hazel's stomach tied itself into knots as she set the water kettle on the electric stove, then worked on building a fire. She wasn't sure what she could say to make this awful discomfort between Bennett and her go away, but it'd become clear that this wasn't going to work itself out unaddressed. Not the way it had when Bennett had come back to Luna after she'd rejected his proposal.

Perhaps this was simply a continuation of that mess?

Likely.

How would this ever work out?

The door creaked as a chilled gust of air stirred against her cheek. Then the latch clicked shut, leaving the fledgling warmth of the fire to touch her skin. Hazel stood and turned to look at Bennett. He'd tugged his stocking cap off and was pulling the sleeves of his coat from his arms. Back turned to her, he hung up his winter gear. Then with fingers combing back that dark wavy hair, he squared to her.

"Water's almost warm." She rubbed her palms down her flannel-lined jeans. "Coffee?"

"No. You still have that cocoa mix I brought last winter?"

"Yes." Hazel moved to retrieve the tin of super-rich peppermint-flavored hot chocolate from the cabinet above her stove.

Bennett beat her to it, and he set the tin on the counter behind her. Warmth enveloped her as her heart skidded sideways.

She missed him. His nearness. The way he smelled like spice and vanilla. The way his gentle touch could make her dizzy in the most delicious way ever. Hazel laid a hand on his flannel and savored the steady rhythm of his heart beating beneath her palm. Slowly, she lifted her eyes to connect with his.

He released the tin and let his hand drift slowly from her shoulder blade down to her waist.

"You still like me, don't you?" Hazel whispered.

"I'm in love with you, Zel." He anchored his other hand on her hip.

"I feel like you've been avoiding me."

The connection of their gazes severed as he looked toward something behind her. "Maybe I have been."

"Bennett." Hazel lifted her hands and slid them along both sides of his jaw. "I keep trying to show you how much I love you."

His eyes closed, and his lips pinned together into a tight line. He nodded. Slowly he stepped back. "I know, Zel." When he looked at her again, the contact felt forced. And like agony. "I love you too. I'm always going to love you."

That sounded like the start of a goodbye. Hazel rolled her fingers into his shirt. "Why does this feel scary, then?"

Bennett visibly swallowed. Then he reached behind him and fished something from his back pocket. The old slider latch from the tack room.

"You think love is like this."

"That's not what I think." Was it?

Bennett flinched. "At least, that's what you think marriage is."

Resentment bubbled from beneath her desperation to make things right between them. "That's not the same thing."

"Maybe it isn't. But the love I have for you . . ." He shook his head and gently pried her hold from his shirt.

"I asked you to move in with me." She stepped forward, closing the gap he'd just opened between them. "You didn't even answer me. Just walked away."

His jaw clenched, and he blinked. "This is the problem, Zel. You and I have different ideas. Different expectations. I'm not going to be your live-in boyfriend."

"Why?"

"Because I have higher expectations for myself now. I think you should have them for me too."

"I don't know what that means."

The teakettle whistled, startling Hazel. Bennett turned, shut off the heat, and moved the pot to the back of the stove. His shoulders rounded, head hung in defeat. After cramming his fingers through his hair, he turned back to her.

"I want the promise, Hazel." With half a step, he narrowed the space between them while his hand warmed her shoulder. "I want the commitment of marriage. Not because I want to trap you but because it would mean that, no matter what, you and I are going to figure out how to fight for love. How to be together. For better or worse, richer or poorer, sickness and in health. It would mean that I'm not my dad. It would mean that I'm not the selfish man I used to be."

"Your dad was married." Hazel knew she shouldn't whisper those words even as they came from her lips.

Bennett winced. His hand fell away, and he took another step back. This time he kept moving away until his backside came up against the table. With a defeated sag, he lowered his weight onto the top and gripped the back of the nearest chair.

After an agonizing stretch of silence, he lifted his gaze to hers again. "I think we need to step back."

Fear raced through her veins. "What does that mean?"

"We need to figure out what we want, both of us, for the future."

"Why can't we just stay the way we are?"

He motioned between them. "You want to stay like this?"

No. Not at all. "That's not what I meant."

"Look. We went from strangers, to near enemies, to fake marriage, back to near enemies, and then straight to lovers." His pale cheeks colored as he spoke. With a long breath, he stood and crossed the floor until he was in front of her again.

Hazel stared at the buttons on his chest. He was breaking up with her. Just a few minutes before, he'd claimed he loved her, that he would always love her. Now he was breaking up with her.

She wanted to weep. Or scream. Or both.

With a bent finger, he lifted her chin until she met those eyes again. There it was—that mix of ache and love. It didn't make sense.

Make it stop!

"Hazel." His voice broke on her name. He rolled his lips together and blinked away the sheen in his eyes. "Maybe we need to find something a little steadier between us."

"Like what?"

"Friendship."

"You want to go back to being just friends."

"We were never friends to begin with." His hands fell to hers, and then he wrapped her fingers in a warm hold. "Let's see if we can find that. Maybe then we'll have some kind of solid foundation to build from. Something that isn't going to collapse every time we have a disagreement."

Hazel shook her head. "Can't we work on that without—"

"We need to step back." Conviction seeped into his quiet voice. He squeezed her hands, leaned in, and kissed her head.

And then . . .

Then he was at the door, gathering his winter things and leaving.

Cold air gusted into the cabin before the door clicked shut. Hazel shivered. Her heart cracked. And her mind turned back to Lewis's words about happiness and peace.

There is no such thing . . .

All her happiness had just walked out that door.

CHAPTER SIX

Hunter leaned over Nathan's shoulder, his concentration fastened on the screen in the boy's hands.

"This is where it gets intense." Nathan's thumbs bounced from spot to spot on his controller as his avatar defended the narrowing space he'd claimed.

Heart hammering to the intensity of the game, Hunter startled when the front door of the lodge smacked shut. He jerked his attention up, mind still captive to the battle Nathan was in on *Black Ops*.

Bennett turned from the front door, stomped his boots on the large rug, and then kicked them off before he strode onto the new, wide-wood plank flooring.

"Hey, buddy." Hunter straightened from his bent position and headed toward Bennett.

Swiping his black stocking cap off his head, Bennett nodded. Though his mouth lifted upward, his eyes held a dark, unhappy dimness. Hunter's mind went immediately back to what Gemma had said earlier—something was wrong between Bennett and Hazel. By the looks of it, whatever that something was hadn't gotten any better that afternoon.

Bennett met Hunter's outstretched hand with his palm. "Just came to collect my crew."

"No rush." Hunter gestured toward the folding table and chairs he'd set up in the nearly finished front room, an invitation to come in and sit. The spot was in front of the fireplace—which glowed orange with a cheerful and effective fire—and just to the side of one of the large windows facing the pond. "Nathan has been teaching me the secrets to success for *Black Ops*, and Gemma and Janie have been lost in wedding plans." Once again Hunter motioned with his hand, this time toward the wide staircase.

Bennett looked toward the second story, then met Hunter's look again. "Thanks for letting them hang with you." He walked to Nathan and patted his brother's shoulder. "We'd best get back down the road. I'm guessing you both have homework, and I told my mom I'd get supper tonight."

Nathan barely acknowledged Bennett. Just a slight nod and he stood, not once taking his concentration off his game.

"Not in the car, bud." Bennett repeated the rule he'd established shortly after the kids had moved to Luna.

Hunter knew there were two reasons for it—one, Nathan missed life because he was so glued to his screen, and Bennett was working to change that. And two, mountain roads demanded attention if one did not want to upchuck.

"Almost at a good hold," Nathan muttered.

A significant improvement to the former scowl-and-refuse-to-comply tactic he'd used in the beginning. That had resulted in a lack of screen for three days, which for a hard-core gamer was close to being locked in the stocks on a frigid mountain night.

Once again Hunter mulled on how things had changed. Good changes.

Maybe not all good.

"Gem, we're leaving," Bennett called, his attention pointed at the staircase. Everything about the man, from his posture to the tightness of his jaw to his lack of eye contact, proclaimed a man worn down.

"It's been a few weeks since we've met for Bible study." Hunter slid his hands into his jeans pockets, the cuffs of his exposed thermal shirt catching on the edges of his belt. "Do you have time to get together this week?"

Bennett lifted his chin enough to nod. "Yeah. I can make something work. Thursday?"

"Sure."

"I'll call José and see if he can hop on FaceTime."

"I'll text John."

Gemma and Janie padded down the gleaming wood stairs, their thick socks muffling their steps.

"Bennett! How was your afternoon?" Gemma's sparkling gaze was both suggestive and hopeful.

"Time to go." Bennett put his hat back on and walked toward the door.

Gemma's shoulders slumped. "Oh. That's not what I hoped for." She looked up at Janie, her eyes sad. "I'll see you in town later?"

"Better." Janie dropped an arm around the girl. "I expect to see you at the café at some point."

"Hope you found your pause, Nathan." Bennett tugged the second of his boots on and opened the front door. "Let's go."

Strained silence accompanied the trio of siblings out the door.

Hunter turned to Janie, finding her gaze following the small group as they walked the length of the front deck. Crossing the room, he pulled her into a hug and kissed her head.

"Any idea what's going on there?" she asked.

"No. But I'll ask Bennett on Thursday."

She nodded, wrapping her arms around his waist.

"Is that what was bothering you earlier?" Hunter asked.

She tipped her chin up and shook her head. "No. I didn't even know . . ." Sighing, she lowered her gaze to his chest. "What kind of a best friend does that make me?"

Hunter slid his hand over the back of her head and pressed her against his flannel shirt. "I didn't know either. Guess we've been pretty wrapped up with us."

She laid her cheek against him. "It's been like this wonderful daze. I'm so happy, Hunter." She leaned back and met his eyes. "I love you so much, and I'm deliriously happy thinking about marrying you."

Love and joy squeezed his chest, so warm and so full it nearly hurt. "Me too."

Those sweet blue eyes sheened. She felt it too, this overwhelming emotion that stole his breath.

"But we have to see them." Determination made her eyebrows fold inward. "We have to care about the people around us. They still matter."

"Yeah." This was the girl he'd fallen for—the one whose soft heart ached with someone else's hurt. The one who wanted good for other people. He cupped her jaw with one hand and caressed her cheek. "I'll talk to Bennett, I promise."

Janie nodded, then gripped his hand and led him to the fireplace. "There's something else."

As he'd guessed. "I was hoping you would tell me what it was."

She dropped her hold and turned toward the window. "A stranger came into the café today—a girl about sixteen, maybe seventeen years old."

"By herself?" Unusual.

Janie nodded.

"Was she lost?"

"No. She came here on purpose." She turned, and when she let him see her eyes again, he found a storm there.

"She came looking for me."

Hunter drew straight. "You? Why?"

Her lips pressed tight. She swallowed. Her brow creased with tight lines. And then she exhaled a shuddered breath. "She says she's my sister."

The words felt strange coming from her mouth. Sister?

Janie had been an only child. Always. She'd never even considered having a sister, because why would she? Anyway, she had Hazel. And Hunter.

She'd never felt lonely for siblings.

Resentment threatened to rise. A sister! Not only had her father up and left them, but he'd gone off and created a whole other life. Didn't even miss them.

Hadn't had one regret.

"Janie." Warm and rough, Hunter's large hand slid down her arm until his fingers latched on to hers. "Come here, sweetie." He led her to one of the rail-back chairs set up at the card table beside the large stone fireplace. There he pulled her down until she perched on one of his legs.

Had it been only a few months ago she'd thought she really only wanted a renewed friendship with this man? Now she sat on his lap, his arm curling around her, pulling her snug. He kissed her temple and tucked her head against his shoulder.

"You have a sister," he whispered, as if trying to decern the reality for himself.

"That's what she says."

"What's her name?"

"Olivia."

"And you're sure what she claims is true?"

Janie lifted her head and sighed. "She was all secretive and antsy until she found out my name—Truitt. Then she stared at me, like she was making sense of a riddle or something. She asked if Mike Truitt was my dad."

Lips pressed, Hunter nodded. "Seems like a genuine claim, then. Did you . . . I mean, I guess I always thought you'd never heard from your dad. But . . ."

"I didn't know." With both her palms pressed to his chest, Janie used him as leverage to stand. There was too much fire in her veins to sit. Too much tension winding her tight. "He left. That was it. Said he wanted a life a little more exciting than this small mountain town. He could have been dead as far as I knew. I thought . . ." Her voice cracked.

Hunter stood again and was right there at her side, strong hand rubbing her back. "Thought what?"

"Thought he didn't want a family. Didn't want kids." She looked up at him, unable to douse the waterworks spilling from her eyes. "Turns out he just didn't want me."

"Oh, Janie." Hunter shook his head. "That can't be right. I can't imagine anyone not wanting you."

Janie tucked herself into the refuge of his arms, her fists clinging to his shoulders. "I don't know what to do with this, Hunt. Why is she here? And why now, of all times? It's like life finally turned the right direction for us, and now this?"

Hunter held her close, one hand caressing her shoulder. "Where is she now?"

Shrugging, Janie sniffed and commanded herself to get ahold of her tumbling emotions. "I'm not sure. I told her to come back to the café tonight. Then I called Tara and asked her to cover for me. I just needed to talk to you."

"She doesn't have a place to stay?" Hunter leaned back, hands covering both her shoulders.

Janie looked to the floor and shook her head. "No. Seems she thought she'd sleep in her car."

"That's not going to be okay."

"I know."

His touch fell from her arms, and she couldn't help but suspect his disappointment. Anyone else, she'd have offered to help. She'd have gone to Mama, and they would have made sure a kid on her own had a safe, warm place to sleep.

That was what they did. It was what *Mama* did.

But Janie hadn't told Mama. She didn't want to tell her.

"Hunter, I can't—"

Gentle brown eyes met her pleading look. Did he wince? Was he upset with her?

"I'll come down tonight, okay?"

"What then?"

"We'll see, I guess."

Janie pulled back. "I need something more definitive than that. I don't think that I can—"

"Janie, you jammed your heart into a freezer because you were mad at me."

She leaned back. "What?"

"I'm not trying to rehash old things that we buried not so long ago. But I'm saying that with me, you were someone else. Someone you're not. Don't go that way again." He cupped her jaw. "You have a beautiful, joyous, tender heart, my love. Don't let the anger with your dad make you ugly toward this girl."

Janie blinked against the burning liquid in her eyes. "I don't even know her, Hunter."

He nodded. "She came here for something. To meet you, for starters. So let's meet her."

Shutting her eyes, Janie let her face tip down. The mild tug of pain in her head that she'd come up there with pulled harder. Wouldn't take long, or much, for it to become a full-blown, throbbing headache.

She didn't think she could do this, even with Hunter at her side.

Hunter's arms enveloped her once again. And once again she was safely tucked against him.

Secure in the refuge he offered.

"I'll be right there with you, sweetheart."

His solemn whispered words were more than a promise—sweet as that may be. They were imperative. He wasn't going to be her way out of this.

Janie puzzled—and maybe smoldered a bit—over why.

CHAPTER SEVEN

ALONE IN THE VAST cabin that had recently been vacated by not only Janie but the work crew as well, Hunter pressed his elbows into his knees as he pondered the latest developments in their some-times-serene mountain world. He pulled his phone out to call John, to seek the older and so-much-wiser man's advice.

But something gave him pause.

So rather than finding John's name and tapping Send, Hunter pressed the phone between both palms, lowered his head, and closed his eyes. "Father . . . wow, God. That still overwhelms me—that I can call You Father." He had to pause there, as emotion stirred his soul. Then he blew out a controlled breath. "Father, I don't know what to do. Janie—how do I help her?"

There, he paused longer. Listening, with his mind and his heart. Waiting, just like John had told him he should do. After a span, and when he still wasn't sure what the right way to go was, he sighed. "You'll show us. Help us—both me and Janie—follow You. And, God? This kid? Olivia? I'm sure she's got a heavy load on her back, or why else would she have come to Luna to find her half sister? So please be with her too. Show us Your way so we can please You. Amen."

Sniffing, Hunter sat up and let his gaze wander outside the wide window, over the frozen lake and toward the hills on the other side. As he let the wonder of the created world calm the thrashing within, the prayer written by Martin Luther that John had sent recently drifted into Hunter's mind. Raising the phone he still held, he flipped through his saved files until he found the one titled "Empty Vessel."

Behold, Lord, an empty vessel that needs to be filled. My Lord, fill it. I am weak in faith; strengthen thou me. I am cold in love; warm me and make me fervent that my love may go out to my neighbor.

I do not have a strong and firm faith; at times I doubt and am unable to trust thee altogether.

O Lord, help me.

Hunter stopped there, though there was half the prayer left to read, and shut his eyes again.

He whispered the last line that he'd read. "O Lord, help me." Emotion clenched his chest again as he wondered that he was not alone. Not ever again.

With renewed hope, though he could not determine the future and still ached for Janie's stricken heart, Hunter stood and stretched. The sun would begin its journey behind the western peaks in quick time. He needed a walk, and he should go talk to his sister.

Clouds had congregated, creating a blanket of gray white over what had been blue hours before. A few flakes of snow drifted lazily from above the trees as Hunter passed his trailer and made his way onto the ridge trail. He tucked his bare hands into his heavy coat, grateful for his warm hat and snug boots.

The brown-tinted snow pack that clearly marked the trail proclaimed its common use—though less so than it had been traveled before he and Janie became engaged. That should not have been so, and Hunter chided himself for allowing it.

Hazel sometimes needed space though. Especially after a longer stretch of continuous socialization—and she'd been neck deep in that sort of thing since Bennett had moved to Luna with his two younger half siblings. It hadn't been entirely unusual for Hazel to disappear for long stretches of time anyway. Add that stress, and . . . well.

Well, nothing. She was his sister. His only living family. He should have checked in with her, no excuses.

His long, quick strides brought him through the pine forest and past the aspen grove as the trail took a sharp descent toward Elk Lake, then opened to a full, pure view of the cabin.

Hunter paused.

The sight still triggered a flurry of mixed reactions. He'd spent the later part of his childhood and all his teenage years in that little box of a cabin. Grown up there with Hazel. And Nan. And Pops.

He'd seen a lot—maybe more than a boy should have seen. Went through some dark, heavy times that still weighed heavy on his soul.

But there had been good times too. Fishing with Hazel. Nan's baking, making that tiny box of a home smell like warm, cinnamon goodness. And sometimes, when Pops was more like his old self, playing cribbage with him. Must have done that more than he thought he had, because Hunter still did math out loud, the way one would count for the game.

A tight corner of his mouth lifted ever so slightly. Good. That was good—to find a fond memory of his grandfather. Hard as it might be, he needed to try harder to sift through the bad to find the good. It *was* there. Starting with when Pops and Nan took Hunter and Hazel in. Even came off the trapline to fight to get Hazel back when, for a short time, the state had determined she shouldn't be in their remote care.

There had been good in Pops. And as Hunter pondered the years that seeped by after his parents' death, he had to admit that Pops's grief was what had stolen so much of the good from the man he'd once been.

Life was hard. Hunter knew that. How did one not go that way though? *O Lord, help me.*

On that silent prayer, he started forward again. At the cabin, he climbed the two steps of the front deck, knocked on the door, and when nothing stirred inside, opened the door and poked his head inside. "Zel?"

No answer. Not really that surprising. Hazel wasn't much for staying indoors unless the weather or the darkness required it. Shutting the door, Hunter wandered down the steps and around to the back of the cabin. A flash of movement in the corral drew his attention.

Little early in the evening for feeding chores, but not terribly so. Maybe he'd be able to help her break the ice near the shore and haul water—something he should make a habit of doing. Why hadn't he thought of that before? Back when they were kids, that had been his job.

Hunter tucked his chilly hands into his pockets as he neared the corral fence. "Hazel."

Her back toward him, Hazel started and then spun around.

Had she really not heard him? Not normal.

As soon as she looked at him, she turned her face away and wiped her cheek with her gloved hand.

Hunter's heart squeezed. "Hey, sis. You okay?"

She straightened, lifted her chin, and met his gaze. "Of course. You just startled me."

"I called for you back at the cabin."

Shrugging, she gave him her back again. "Didn't hear you."

Hunter let that anomaly go unaddressed as he passed through the gate and moved to her side. "What are you doing?" He truly wondered, because with a quick survey, he could see she wasn't in the middle of feeding chores. No buckets out. Hayfork must still be on its peg inside the tack room. No carefully measured grain in the wooden feed trough.

Back still stubbornly to him, Hazel simply held something up above her shoulder for his inspection.

Hunter took it from her grasp. "What's this?"

"The old slide lock." She nodded toward the door.

Oh. Yeah, that sure was what the thing was. He shifted his attention from the worn block of wood in his hand to the door Hazel stared at. There he found a shiny new latch system. One that would have had to have been ordered special and would have taken some time and effort to install.

"Bennett do this?"

Hazel sniffed. "Yeah."

This was not adding up. Bennett had been upset when he'd picked up the kids to go back down to town. Hazel stood like a zombie, staring at that new latch. Sniffing. Not looking at Hunter, because she somehow believed he wouldn't know that she'd been crying if she didn't make eye contact.

"That was nice of him." He edged closer to Hazel.

"Yeah."

"So that means those tears are of gratitude?"

From her profile, he could see her jaw clench.

Knowing Hazel was just as likely to throw an elbow in his gut as she was to accept the gesture, Hunter wrapped an arm around her shoulder anyway. "Talk to me, Zel."

She exhaled a shuddering breath, stiffened for a heartbeat, and then folded into his side. "He said he doesn't want me to feel trapped ever again."

Hunter lifted the old slide lock, as if measuring against the new latch. "This should have been done a long time ago." He passed the block back to her. "I should have been the one to do it. I'm sorry."

Hazel took the old piece of hardware and flung it toward the long stack of firewood on the lee side of the structure.

"Zel." Hunter turned, and grasping her shoulders, he forced her to turn as well. "You and me, we're good. We're on the same side now, remember?"

Her tight lips trembled. She nodded.

"Tell me why you're upset about this."

"I'm not."

"Lies."

"Not about this."

"Then what?"

She winced, like she was trying really hard to bury the emotion that was torturing her. When she couldn't, she crossed her arms tight and swallowed. "Bennett . . ." And there, she broke. Her shoulders shook as she caved in on herself.

Hunter had never seen this from Hazel. Not once.

His heart broke, and a flare of anger streaked clean through him. Bennett. He'd trusted the man. What had he done to his sister? "What about Bennett?"

"He said we needed to step back."

Though Hunter had a hunch that was the case, the blow still hit him with shock. "He broke up with you?"

She pressed the heel of her palm against her cheek and swiped away the rolling tears, as if they were offensive. "I don't know. He says he still loves me, but he wants to step back. But I don't even know what that means."

"Me either." What was Bennett thinking? Was this because Hazel wouldn't marry him?

Surely this wasn't Bennett's way of changing her mind, was it?

"How can he do that?" Hazel asked.

The breathy, choked quality of Hazel's voice tore at Hunter's heart even more. He pulled her into a full hug. Glancing at the door latch that Bennett had replaced, Hunter forced his mind past the reactionary anger toward the other man who had hurt his sister and worked to untangle the mystery.

He didn't want her to feel trapped. So he let her go?

Seemed . . . well, maybe logical. But harsh nonetheless. "I'll talk to him."

Hazel tugged away. "No. I don't want you to. I didn't even want you to know."

"Zel, everyone will know. Luna's small. And to tell you the truth, the kids were just telling me this afternoon that something was wrong between you and Bennett. They already know."

"So I'm to be humiliated, not just brokenhearted?"

"I very much doubt that's Bennett's intention." The man wasn't cruel. But this did seem extreme. And unkind.

"Good thing I'm used to being up here. Alone."

Knife to his chest. "You're not alone, Zel."

She sighed, tipped her head against his shoulder, and remained silent.

It didn't matter if she said anything though. Hunter was going to talk to Bennett, even if she didn't want him to. Right after he met this girl who claimed to be Janie's sister.

Man. It had been a busy day after all.

CHAPTER EIGHT

BENNETT WALKED THE CREEK-SIDE trail until the light of the sun disappeared behind the western hills. The cloud cover made what remained of the day gray, which seemed appropriate. Everything within him felt gray.

His phone vibrated inside his pocket. With a couple of clicks, he read Hunter's text.

Need to talk. Tonight.

Not that surprising. Even so, Bennett blew out a long breath of discouragement and frustration. He didn't want to talk about Hazel and him and their relationship status. Hadn't even wanted to change it in the first place.

He clicked on his flashlight app to finish the last twenty yards of the trail that would lead him to the parking lot where he'd left his car. Once there Bennett leaned his backside against the driver's-side door, rather than climbing inside and cranking up the heater.

Tipping his head back, he gazed at the inky darkness that clamped over the valley. He clicked his flashlight off, and the blackness swallowed him.

He still felt it. That stirring of panic left over from his childhood.

"You're fine, Benji." Hazel's hand covered his, then her palm warmed the edge of his jaw as she turned his face toward the white glow of the moon. *"Focus here."*

The light of the moon had eased the clawing fear that night. That, and the steady touch of the woman he'd believed at the time was his wife.

Now, there was only darkness. No moon. No warm hand. No wife. A shiver ran through his core. "I am afraid," he whispered into the cold night.

Not just of the darkness, though it truthfully did still bother him.

Afraid he'd lose Hazel. Forever. Afraid that every step he took was wrong and that he'd never find his way out of the messes of his life's choices.

Warm liquid rimmed his eyelids, and he swallowed against the overwhelming sense of loss and helplessness. Blinking his eyes open, Bennett tried to see into the thick night. A cold dot landed on his cheek, quickly melting against his skin. Another fell onto his nose, then another onto his chin.

Snow.

Somehow he found comfort in the sensation. He couldn't see it in the darkness, but there it was. He could feel it.

Shoving his hands into his coat pockets, Bennett shut his eyes again and leaned into the sense of touch as the flakes continued to kiss his face.

"I'm trying to follow You, you know?" A tear leaked from the corner of one eye, the warm liquid a contrast to the cold.

A fresh shiver rattled through his middle again, but in its wake, a calm settled. Undefined and yet just like the snowflakes melting on his skin, Bennett felt it.

He felt Him.

Hunter arrived just like he'd said, slipping through the back kitchen door at nearly eight that evening.

The dining room held a sparse smattering of people—most of Janie's customers had enjoyed their black-eyed-pea soup and hearty rye bread, with a side of kale and cranberry salad, and had gone home before the snow piled up. Three patrons remained—Jeremy and Leslie Yates, who were enjoying a night out without their two kids and were thus lingering over their decaf coffee and caramel apple crumble—and Olivia ... presumably Truitt.

"That her?" Hunter stopped at the sink where Janie was depositing an empty pan, kissed her temple, and went straight for the door that separated the kitchen from the retail dining room. His gaze pointed through the window in the door.

Janie snatched a towel for her wet hands and walked over to him. "Yes."

At a table in the corner, away from the big window and on the opposite of the dining room from the Yates', Olivia sat alone, staring at her half-eaten bowl of soup.

"I'm going to talk to her," Hunter said.

"No." Janie placed her hand over his before he could push open the door. "Wait for me—and until Jeremy and Leslie are done."

Hunter looked down at her with a scowl.

"You'll scare her, Hunt." She pressed her thumb against the twin lines just above his nose. "Especially with this glare. What's that all about, anyway? You weren't this worked up about her this afternoon. In fact, you were the one who told me to be gentle and kind."

Hunter took her hand and lowered it from his face. "I *was* concerned. And I am still. For both of you. But . . ." He drew in a long breath, then pointed to his still-lined brow. "This is probably from the conversation I had with Hazel."

"Oh." Janie felt dread plunge through her middle. "That bad, huh?"

"Bennett broke up with her."

"What?"

Hunter ran his fingers through his hair, making what desperately needed to be cut a crazy mess. He looked like a wild bear of a man, with his deep frown, emotion-intense eyes, and that thick brown hair sticking out every which way.

Janie reached to fix what she could—which was the hair and not much else. "Did they have a fight?"

"Doesn't sound like it. He came up and replaced that old slide lock on the shed so that you can open or shut it from the outside and the *inside*. Told her he didn't want her to feel trapped ever again." There he stopped, lifting his brows to emphasize the double meaning in that, in case Janie missed it.

She hadn't missed it. But she didn't need to say so.

Hunter continued. "Then he told her he thought they needed to step back."

Janie blinked. That seemed so . . . delayed, if she was being honest. Seemed like something Bennett would have done months back, right after Hazel had turned down his marriage proposal. Why hadn't he done it then but decided to now?

She ran her thumb along the cool band of her diamond ring. "You don't think it's because of us, do you?"

"Us? What would we have anything to do with it?"

She held up her ring finger. "Because we're engaged. Maybe it triggered something in Bennett. Resentment or something."

Hunter's shoulders sagged, and his scowl turned thoughtful. "I don't know. Resentment seems out of character for him . . . I just don't know. But I'm going to find out."

"You are?"

"I'm going to talk to him after I make sure everything here is okay."

Janie glanced at the dining room just as Jeremy and Leslie stood and put on their coats. "Olivia is just a kid. I can handle it." She looked back at Hunter. "Go talk to your friend. But be nice. Remember, he *is* your friend."

"He kind of wrecked my sister's heart, so . . ." He blew out a frustrated breath. "But that's going to have to wait. I'm not leaving until I hear what Olivia has to say."

"I'll be okay, Hunt."

He shook his head, claiming both of her hands. "You and me. We do life together. That's what this is and what it's going to be from here on out, Janie."

As he pressed a kiss to her forehead, warmth curled through her chest. She did love this man fiercely. Might be why she'd been so extremely, stupidly mad at him—all that fierceness aimed the wrong way. Janie tipped up on her toes to catch his lips with hers. "I like that. Me and you, from here on out."

The scowl carving his forehead smoothed. That was better. Much better to go talk to Olivia. "Ready?" She continued to hold one of his hands as she moved to go into the dining room.

"I am if you are." He shouldered the door open, waited for her to pass, and then followed.

"How's the soup?" Janie stopped at the table where the young woman sat. The girl wore a white stocking cap that contrasted beautifully with her dark hair.

Dark, like Janie's. Olivia had blue eyes, like Janie's too.

Olivia shrugged. "Never had it before."

"Split pea is a staple here," Janie said. "Especially in the winter."

Hunter dropped Janie's hand and held out an offer of a handshake. "Hunter Wallace. Olivia, is it?"

The girl looked at him with a stony expression. Then she raised her brow and shifted her eyes back to Janie. "He a cop?"

"No." Janie slid into a chair across from Olivia. "My fiancé."

"Why'd you bring him into this?"

"I just told you. He's my fiancé. Of course I told him that a stranger came into my café who turned out to be my never-heard-of half sister."

Olivia watched with obvious suspicion as Hunter lowered into a chair beside Janie.

"Let's start there, how about?" Hunter said.

"Start what?"

"Your story." Hunter sounded military. Or like a cop. Sharp. Direct. And a little cold. "How do you know Janie is your sister?"

"I didn't. Not when I came into the café anyway. But then she said her name, and that's how I know."

"But you came up to Luna looking for me," Janie said.

"Yes."

"Why?"

Olivia pressed her lips together and fiddled with the spoon in her half-full soup bowl. "I wanted to see what you were like."

"I didn't even know I had a sister. How did you know?"

"Dad." She lifted her eyes only enough to glance at Janie, then focused on the table. "When he was on a binge, he said something about having a daughter in Luna."

Janie glanced at Hunter, catching his wince. She looked down at her folded hands and let that sink in. Binge . . . Did that mean her dad was—

"Where is your dad?"

"In a rehab center for the third time. Court order."

Janie's stomach twisted. "Alcohol?"

Olivia nodded.

Pain clenched in Janie's chest as she looked to Hunter. His hand slid across her shoulders until his arm settled around her. He knew what this news was doing to her. Knotting her insides and stabbing her heart. He knew, because he'd lived it himself.

Likely, his empathy covered not just Janie's pain but Olivia's too. Because the girl sitting across from them had lived through it too. Right up there with a front-row experience.

Janie cleared her throat. "What about your mom?"

With a shrug, Olivia slouched back. "She's at home."

"Does she know where you are?" Hunter asked.

"She knows I'm in the mountains."

"That's vague." Removing his arm from Janie's shoulders, Hunter leaned forward, settling his arms on the table. "And not good enough."

Defiance lit Olivia's blue eyes when she lifted them to meet Hunter's stare. "What's it to you?"

"How old are you, Olivia? Sixteen?"

"Seventeen."

"Seventeen, and over a thousand miles from home. In the mountains in the dead of winter by yourself." He leaned back and folded his arms. "Do you have any money?"

"That's none of your business."

"It is now, because if you're Janie's sister like you're claiming, then you're family. And it's my business because a young woman sleeping alone in her car on a freezing winter's night isn't acceptable no matter who you are. What about a place to stay? Do you have that figured out?"

"I *am* Olivia Truitt. You can check my license." She dug out her phone from her coat pocket and flashed the license at Hunter.

He read it, nodded, but didn't let up. "And a place for the night?"

Olivia swallowed and shot Janie a meek look. "I . . . I was going to . . ."

Janie shook her head. "We already talked about not sleeping in your car earlier today. You'll freeze to death. Literally."

A tense silence grew.

"I didn't really think about the cold. It's not . . . I mean, in Austin we barely ever see snow, so . . ."

Janie nodded. "We can help you, Olivia. But we need to know why your mom doesn't know where you are and why you decided to drive by yourself all the way up here without a plan."

"Livy," the girl said. "I go by Livy. And I told my mom that I was going on a ski trip with the youth group I've been going to with my boyfriend." She peeked at them, a hint of that defiance still lingering in her expression. "They are going on a ski trip, by the way. Just . . . not here."

"Big Sky?"

She nodded.

Janie exhaled a fraction of relief. At least Livy had people she knew sort of close by.

"Last month," Olivia admitted.

Oh. So much for relief.

"The first thing you need to do, then, is call your mom." Hunter folded his arms across his chest. "Let her know where you are and that you're safe."

Olivia eyed him.

Janie reached across the table. "You are safe, Livy. Like I said, we'll help you."

"Back to the other question. Do you have money?"

"Why?"

Janie shot Hunter a scowl. "That sounded bad."

"I didn't mean it that way." Hunter eyed Janie, then looked back at Livy. "I just want to know how you planned to get back to Texas."

"I have around forty dollars left."

Thirty-six, according to the quick count Janie had done earlier. But she didn't need to speak up right then.

"Forty dollars?" Hunter shook his head. "That will maybe get you to Colorado. With a good tail wind. What were you thinking?"

A sheen glazed over her eyes. "I didn't know how much gas it would take to get here. Or how cold snow actually is. I had to buy this back in Colorado Springs." She tugged on her white winter coat. "I found it at a Goodwill off the interstate."

Hunter nodded, the intensity in his posture easing. "You picked a good one. And that was smart to look at a thrift store."

"They had boots too. I have them in my car."

"Good." A half smile eased onto his mouth.

Janie took in the depth of Hunter's concern, and a flush of love ran anew through her veins. It probably looked like nosy pushiness to Olivia, but Janie knew better. Hunter wanted to know that this kid was safe—and he would see that she was, whether she was really Janie' half sister or not.

Hunter was *that* man, and it made her proud.

"Back to calling your mom, letting her know where you are . . ."

Olivia crumbled. "My phone is dead, and my charger isn't working. And it wouldn't matter anyway. My mom *should* be in a rehab center too."

The twist in Janie's gut was twice as hard as the first had been. Her dad and her mom?

God, why are people so messed up?

Life could be pretty painful. And then it could be bleak. Without God, without real hope in Jesus, what else was there?

Plenty. Lots of ways to try to smother the aching emptiness, that was. Anger, bitterness. That had been Janie's chosen method. But there were other options. Drugs and alcohol seemed to be popular. Thing was, there were lots of ways to *try* to cover up the need.

None of them filled it. Not ever.

"Janie and I both have phones." Hunter's tone had switched decidedly from firm and a little too authoritative to gentle and compassionate. "Call your mom, Livy."

"After that we'll get you settled upstairs in my apartment," Janie said.

Hunter's hand warmed her shoulder, then squeezed. Janie glanced at him and found a veiled warning in his look.

"How about we have some of your caramel apple crumble," he said. "Pretty sure I spotted some left in the kitchen."

Olivia hadn't even finished her soup. Janie furrowed her eyebrows at Hunter.

He stood. "I'll give you a hand." He motioned with his head toward the kitchen, then glanced at Olivia. "Ice cream on yours?"

"Sure."

Hunter nodded, waited for Janie to stand, and then took her hand as he led her to the kitchen. As soon as the door swayed shut behind them, he turned to her. "I don't know about this, Janie."

"What?"

"It's one thing to help a stranger. Feed her. But . . . have her stay with you in your apartment?"

"Where else is she going to stay?"

"The Cedar Inn isn't that expensive."

"It isn't great either."

"Neither is having a total stranger sleep in your apartment while you're there alone."

"She's my sister."

"So she says."

"Why would she lie about that?"

Hunter ran his hand along the back of his neck. "I just don't like it. Maybe we can go talk to Mama B. She has a couple of spare rooms. I could stay in one and—"

"No." Janie wasn't about to do that, and no amount of argument from Hunter was going to sway her on that.

"Why not? Mama B is always—"

"Mike is her ex-husband. I'm not going to walk into my mom's home with Mike's secret daughter in tow and ask her to give the kid a room for the night."

Hunter stared at Janie, as if working through that scenario from her point of view. After a moment he shook his head. "I think your mom will be okay."

"I don't." Janie crossed her arms. "I'm not springing this on her and then asking her to house Olivia without a chance to process it."

"You just found out."

"Yeah, and remember how upset I was this afternoon?"

He pressed his lips together.

"I know. Mama is a better person than I am, but—"

"I didn't say that." Hunter clasped her hand. "And I don't think it. I just don't like the idea of you upstairs spending the night with a stranger in the apartment. It doesn't sit well."

"I'll leave the door unlocked and my phone on."

He shook his head. "That's not a whole lot of comfort."

"You could stay at Mama's."

"What excuse would I give her for that?"

Janie shrugged. "You'll think of something."

He sighed. "Don't leave your door unlocked. Just give me a key."

"It's hanging in the pantry." Janie pointed toward the back of the kitchen.

Hunter scowled. "Janie."

"What?"

"It's bad enough you leave the kitchen unlocked half the time . . ."

"I lock my apartment. Usually."

Hands scrubbing his face, Hunter groaned.

"It's Luna," Janie said.

"There are sketchy people all over the world."

"I've been fine so far."

For several heartbeats Hunter stared at her with stern disapproval. Then with a drop of his shoulders, he relented. "Fine. I'll stay at Mama B's. And you'll keep your phone *in your hand* at all times." He pulled her against him and wrapped her with both arms. "I just want to take this moment to tell you, yet again, that we should have eloped. It would have made this whole situation a whole lot easier."

Janie snuggled against him, slipping her arms around his waist. "No arguments on that." Then she tipped her chin up and rested it on his chest. "But it'll be worth the wait."

He dropped a kiss onto the tip of her nose. "You're worth everything." Then he moved to dish the promised apple crumble. "Just so you know though"—he leaned to whisper near her ear—"this waiting is killing me."

A delicious warmth pooled in her belly as tiny, thrilling sparks shot through her. She leaned into him, kissed his cheek, and whispered, "Me too."

CHAPTER NINE

BENNETT PUT THE LAST of the dishes he'd washed in the cabinet, his mind still up the hill at the cabin. How could he make Hazel understand?

The sheen of tears in her eyes destroyed his heart, and even the memory of her devastated expression wrecked him. More, he could see her point of view. Hadn't he just told her, when he'd moved to Luna, that he aimed to prove her belief in his fragile love wrong?

And here he was, telling her they needed to step back. Find a stable friendship.

Thing was, he did love her still. Wildly. So much that it was tempting to ignore his conscience telling him to take things in a different direction for now.

For now.

He sure hoped that was the case.

A pounding on the front door jarred Bennett out of his mental maze. With a start, he straightened the stack of white plates he'd placed on the open shelf, then turned to wipe his hands on a kitchen towel. From the front room, he could hear Gemma answer the door.

". . . hey, Hunter. I get to see you twice in one day!"

"I'm a lucky guy that way."

Bennett could imagine his friend tugging one of Gemma's boxer braids.

"Bennett around?"

"Yep. In the kitchen. Still grumpy."

As far as Bennett could tell, Hunter didn't respond to that.

Bennett had enough time to jam his hands through his hair, brushing the wild nearly black waves that had grown too long out of his eyes before Hunter strode into the kitchen.

"Hey, Hunt."

"Bennett." Hunter speared him with a sharp look. "We need to talk."

With a long-drawn breath, Bennett plunged his hands into his jeans pockets and leaned against the counter. No guessing games as to what this was about. "Yeah. That's probably a good idea."

Hunter glanced over his shoulder. "The kids know what's going on?"

"They know things are . . . not great."

Hunter's frown deepened. "They know you broke up with my sister?"

Bennett's shoulders collapsed. He'd hoped Hunter would understand. Have his back. It'd been a farfetched hope, since Hazel was his little sister and he was fiercely protective of her.

"Talk to me, Bennett."

He met Hunter's glare, then nodded toward the small high-top round table in the far corner of the galley kitchen. Hunter followed him, and both men sat.

Bennett pressed his arms against the edge of the table. "I didn't want to—and I don't know that breaking up with her is exactly the right way to say it."

"You told her you wanted to be friends."

"Yeah, something like that."

"That's a breakup, my man."

Hunter slumped back against the chair. "I know . . . but it isn't because that's what I want."

"You're not making a whole lot of sense."

"It's like this. Hazel and I, we're this roller coaster of crazy emotion. We couldn't stand each other at first, then all the sudden we were married—sort of. Then I find out she lied about that, and we're back to loathing. Next thing I know, I can't stop thinking about her—missing her—and then she shows up on a busy Chicago sidewalk telling me she's sorry and misses me too." Bennett took a breath and shook his head. "We're all highs and lows. Fire and ice." He caught Hunter's stare and held it. "Does that seem like something that's going to last?"

The heat in Hunter's expression cooled. After a moment of consideration, he dipped a nod. "I see where you're coming from."

"Seems like if we can't figure out something more stable, we don't have a chance."

"I don't know if Hazel's going to get that."

Once again, defeat pressed down on Bennett's shoulders. "I know."

"This just seems like it came out of the blue." Hunter leaned forward. "My sister loves you, Bennett. I know she's awkward and stubborn, but she—"

"I know that. And I love her. Honest, Hunter, I do." Bennett looked up again. "But Thanksgiving night—after you proposed to Janie?"

Hunter nodded.

"She asked me to move in with her. Like that would make the piercing reminder of her rejection better. Like it would be good enough."

Rolling his lips together, Hunter sighed. "I'm sorry, man."

At least he got that—what Hazel's backhanded offer had done to Bennett. "Things between us since have been . . . tense, to say the least. I can't get past it—that the best she sees me as is live-in-boyfriend material. I don't know what else to do. We can't move forward, not the way we're going—which is clearly the wrong way. I don't want things to end. I've prayed and agonized over the whole thing. Knowing that most of it is my own fault. This is what I've been pressed with. Step back and find a friendship. Build something that has a chance to last."

For several awkward moments, Hunter simply stared at his hands. "I remember you telling me that you didn't know how to step back—didn't think it would work."

Bennett snorted a derisive chuckle. "You can see how well it's going."

Hunter's face lifted, and he pinned Bennett with demand. "If you want it to, you're going to have to be the one to make it work. At least at first. Hazel's a fight-or-flight kind of woman. And she's had almost zero practice with sorting through life's mazes with other people. In truth, she works harder at understanding her dogs than she ever has at getting people."

Bennett nodded. "I know. I intend to do everything I can."

Another spell of hard silence spanned.

"Hunt?"

"Yeah."

"Was it really impossible for you to be Janie's friend?"

At that, Hunter dropped back in his chair and sighed. "I didn't do great at it. Obviously. It was worse because every time I thought of her dating Grady, I went a little nuts. But I did try. Maybe you'll have to ask Janie. But I get what you're saying about stability. And the truth is, Janie and I were friends first. Back before we were engaged and broke up. She'd been my best friend. So it does make sense. I think it's just going to be harder for you doing things this way."

"You mean backward?"

He shrugged. "A little bit, I guess."

"There's another issue. A bigger one."

Hunter nodded, as if he knew where this one was going.

"We don't have the same faith foundation."

"You mean she doesn't know Jesus."

"Yeah." Bennett's sore heart squeezed with a fresh ache—a blend of sadness for her and hopelessness for them. "I didn't realize how important that would be. Though I was taught about Jesus when I was young, I left the faith as little more than a kid. Sharing core beliefs didn't seem important to me until now. Until I've found myself in love with a woman who doesn't share mine. It's like we're not going the same way."

Swallowing visibly, Hunter nodded again. "I don't know what to tell you on that. With Janie and me—she was the one with the faith before. But when we broke up, that wasn't the issue. Not that I think it wouldn't have become an issue at some point, because I can see now that it probably would have eventually gone that way. That's just not what happened between us—why we fell apart."

"Do you think you would have believed eventually, if you'd stayed together? Maybe because of her faith?"

Hunter sat still, then leveled a sad look on Bennett. "I can't say either way for sure. I have a gut feeling that the answer would have been no—or that things would have been pretty hard. Looking back, I think I needed some isolation. To feel the desperate need for God without something to smother it with. Janie . . . She was everything to me. After she found out about Pops, she just stepped into that void. Became my crutch in life. When she wouldn't go with me into the navy, it was like ripping off a bandage and finding out the wound was much worse than I'd ever thought. If that makes any sense."

Bennett nodded. It was what he'd been afraid of. These past several months, he'd been hoping that Hazel would see his faith—and his changed life—and want the same thing in her own life. That she'd want salvation. Hadn't worked that way. Maybe it did for some, but it hadn't for him and Hazel.

Where did that leave him?

"Bennett."

He lifted the focus he'd pinned on his hands back to Hunter.

"God reached me, you know?"

Clamping his jaw, Bennett nodded.

"All things are possible."

Bennett nodded. "Sometimes God's answer is *no* though." He knew from painful experience. He'd begged God as a boy not to let his dad leave. His dad had not only left, but he'd done it with a level of self-justified arrogance that had left Bennett in utter devastation. And seething in resentment.

Hunter's expression strained, as though wrestling with the emotions of that possibility. Made sense—Hazel was his sister, and Bennett knew that Hunter wanted good things for his sister. Beginning with salvation.

"I think John would say the best weapon for that battle is prayer."

Truth. "José would say *amen* to that."

"So we pray." Hunter dropped his feet to the floor and stood. "I'll be doing that battle with you. For Hazel. And for you, my man."

Bennett tried to grab on to the hope Hunter's promise offered. Under the weight of defeat though, it didn't feel like much help.

Hunter gripped Bennett's arm. "I'll talk to her. See if I can help her understand."

"I appreciate that." Though Bennett doubted Hazel would listen. He stood and clapped Hunter's shoulder. "And your prayers."

"You're like a brother to me, Bennett."

Bennett raised his eyes and met Hunter's honest gaze. Hope felt a little more . . . helpful. "Same."

That was something—Hunter's steady friendship. A gift. And a reminder, yet again, that he wasn't alone.

Like the moonlight cutting through the darkness. He just needed to focus on the light.

Janie's apartment had always been her refuge. She'd moved into it two months after she and Hunter had broken up—Mama telling her that she needed to find a new direction in her life because she wasn't going to allow her to sour in self-pity.

Janie had done some souring anyway, but not because Mama hadn't tried. That was all on herself.

But that night, as she made up the couch for Olivia, the space felt more like detention than her cozy home where she could relax.

Didn't help that Livy stood off to the side, out of the way, like a cement statue. Watching Janie's every move. Creeping her out a bit.

Maybe Hunter had been right. This wasn't a good idea . . .

With a glance toward the wisp of a girl at the edge of the couch, Janie brushed away the anxiety. Livy was a kid. A lost kid with what sounded like a wreck of a home life. She was harmless. And likely every bit as edgy about meeting Janie as Janie was about discovering she had a sister.

"Want to help me by putting on those pillowcases?" Janie nodded toward the two pillows she'd retrieved from the storage closet.

Olivia shrugged. "Sure." With a snap, she unfolded one case, slipped it over the fluffy bulge, then did the next one.

Janie finished tucking in the covers around the couch cushions. "There. Should be snug as a bug. But if you get cold, there are a few extra blankets in that locker." She pointed to the large leather-covered box in the middle of the floor—the one that doubled as her coffee table.

"Thanks."

"Did you bring clothes to sleep in?"

Olivia slipped the strap of her backpack off her shoulders. "I have some sweats."

Did she pack anything else? Janie ran a quick inspection over the outfit Olivia was wearing. A gray tee with an armadillo imposed on an image of Texas, ripped skinny jeans, and a pair of worn leopard-print slip-on Vans.

"How about a change of clothes for tomorrow?"

"I'm good." Olivia chewed on her thumbnail and looked toward the wall to her left.

That was a no then. "I think I have a few things that might work for you. They'd be warmer, and we can run your stuff through the wash."

The girl dropped her hand as her jaw clamped.

"Olivia?"

"Just Livy."

"Okay, Livy. Did you think through this plan past get in your car and start driving?"

Yet another shrug.

"Sweetie, you've got to think about the next thing. Hunter and I want to help you, but I need to know what you hoped to find here."

"I told you. I hoped to find my sister. That would be you, apparently."

"Okay." A strange mix of puzzlement and honor twisted inside Janie. If she'd been the one to discover she had a half sister somewhere across the map, she wasn't so sure she'd hop in the car, sans any sort of solid plan, to go find her. Then again, Janie wasn't exactly adventurous. What was driving this girl? "Why did you need to find me right away? I mean, it seems impetuous."

"I don't know what that big fancy word means. But when I found out there was someone else out there who shared my DNA, I guess I hoped—"

Janie waited. Livy stared at a spot on the rug halfway across the room.

"Hoped what, Liv?"

"Hoped that maybe it wouldn't be me against the world anymore."

Oh dear. That sounded terribly sad. And a little desperate. Janie lowered onto the thick black-and-white plaid comforter she'd just tucked tight and patted the spot next to her. "You against the world sounds pretty . . . dramatic."

"It is what it is." Livy sat in the spot Janie had indicated but kept herself erect and stiff. "Look, by the looks of your life, I don't expect you to understand—I mean you have your own business and this apartment and a super-hot fiancé and everything—but I've got to figure things out for myself. And if I don't want to end up like my parents—which I don't—I've got to do it quick. Hearing that I had a sister—one who might just be doing okay—it was like this life raft or something. I needed to come see if you were different."

"Different how?"

"Not . . . failing."

"Failing?"

"A drunk. A junkie." Livy winced. "You know."

Janie took that in and said a quick, silent prayer for help. "I'm not either of those—and neither is Hunter. We might understand hard things a little more than you think though. I mean, my dad took off when I was a kid. Said he needed adventure in his life and didn't want to be stuck in this boring small town forever. Basically, my mom and me weren't enough for him anymore." Janie paused to swallow back the resentment, careful not to let it flow in Livy's direction. Their dad's choices weren't Livy's fault. "And Hunter—he lost both his parents to an accident when he was young. His grandparents raised him and his sister—and his grandfather dealt with his son's death by drinking . . . That didn't end well."

Livy rolled her fists tight. "Great. So everyone ends up a wreck." Emotion blazed from her blue eyes when she turned them up to Janie. "Is that just how life is? We're doomed and there's no way out?"

God, let that not be the truth. Not for Janie or Hunter or Livy. Not for Bennett and his two siblings. Not for Hazel.

How did they break free of the chaos?

Janie let her attention drift toward the window to her left. Through the frost-edged glass panes, the darkness was broken by the cool dim light of the waxing moon—light that caught the specs of falling snow, making them glitter.

Long lay the world, in sin and error pining.

The words to the Christmas song "O Holy Night" sang softly in her mind.

"Not everyone," Janie whispered.

A thrill of hope...

She turned and focused on Livy.

The weary world rejoices.

A wave of warmth flooded Janie's heart, washing away the carefully kept reserve she had cradled the moment Livy had proclaimed she was her sister. In the place of that cool resentment, love grabbed hold. A sister! She had a sister.

One who yearned for hope. For a life that wasn't all selfish chaos and destruction. Janie reached across the space between them and covered Livy's clenched hand.

"There is life, Liv. Hopeful and joyful."

With folded brows, Livy turned her reserved gaze to Janie. For several heartbeats she simply studied Janie, as if looking for that hope. Or for a lie.

"Do you know the Christmas story?" Janie asked.

The sense of expectation fell as Livy looked away. "Doesn't everyone? Some baby born in a barn. Joy to the world and all . . . And somehow that led to a tale of a jolly old man in red flying around the world with presents." Livy sent a scowl toward Janie. "I outgrew stocking stories and fairy tales when I was seven."

"That baby wasn't just any baby—his name is Jesus. And He came to break the darkness that holds us captive. The darkness that makes everyone and everything a wreck."

"He didn't do a very good job of it." Livy huffed. "Look, I don't know how we ended up talking about religion and myths. What I really want is to sleep. Maybe then I can think straight."

Disappointment swallowed Janie, but she nodded. "Okay." She pointed toward her bedroom. "You're welcome to use my room to change, and just leave your clothes in there. Including your shoes.

I'll run them through the wash when I get up—which is really early, by the way. I'll be careful not to wake you when I head down to the kitchen."

Livy stood up and snagged her backpack, then started for the bedroom. At the open door, she paused and turned back to Janie. Her expression had softened, and once again she looked like a lost kid who needed a whole lot of hope.

A whole lot of Jesus.

"Thanks," Livy whispered.

"Of course." Janie stood. "You're family, right?"

"I have a feeling you would take care of me even if I wasn't." With that, Livy turned and closed the door.

CHAPTER TEN

"ARE YOU COMING THIS afternoon?"

Hazel startled at the sound of her brother's voice behind her. She lowered the rifle she'd nestled into her shoulder, careful to click on the safety as she pointed the barrel toward the ground. "Seems like you should know better than to sneak up on an armed woman."

Hunter grinned. "Probably. You've never missed what you've intended to hit though. Don't think I'm on your target list." He winked. "Anymore."

"I've missed." Hazel tucked away the smile that threatened her otherwise serious expression. "As to the other . . . you're not on the list. At the moment."

Hunter moved his easygoing look from Hazel toward the target. "That's new."

"A recent acquisition, yes."

"Not your normal practice sheet." He stepped closer to the firing range that was on the opposite side of the cabin from the horse corral. "You usually use the red centers."

"These are standard in the biathlon competition."

Hunter swiveled his head to shoot her a curious look. "You thinking of competing?"

Hazel shook her head. "Not me. Nathan texted me the other day, asking about biathlons. Wanted to know if I knew anything about them. I don't, really. But I know how to ski and I know how to shoot, and it seems like if Nathan's interested in it, we could learn together."

A slow, wide grin lifted Hunter's expression. "Look at you."

"What?"

"That's really thoughtful, Zel. And a great idea." He stepped back to her and landed an arm around her shoulder. "I'm proud of you."

Hazel shouldered him away, feeling both self-conscious and pleased at her brother's praise. "It's not that selfless, you know. Sounds fun, actually. And just so you know, you'll be helping me clear a course. I think we'll need a 3k loop with elevation change and a small 150-meter penalty loop for misses."

"The trapline?"

"That's what I'm thinking. It's already established, follows the upper creek, and we can cut a section to lead here, to the shooting range."

Hunter squeezed her. "I like it. Might need to extend it around the ridge trail for a full 3k." He paused, then cleared his throat. "Have you discussed this with Bennett?"

Hazel stepped out of his reach, walking the fifty meters to retrieve the target, which was notably more expensive than her regular practice targets. At the firing mark—simply a straight aspen log perpendicular to the target at fifty meters—she stopped to gather her ammo and the gloves she'd pulled off earlier.

"Zel?"

"Not yet." She finally met Hunter's gaze, which she'd felt following her as she'd moved. "I planned to today. At the lodge."

Though his grin had faded, Hunter nodded, his look still proud. "So you're coming."

"Yes."

"Good." Hunter shoved his hands into his coat pocket. "This friendship thing with Bennett . . . it's important to him. You're going to try, right?"

Hazel blinked, rubbing her stinging nose. "I have to, don't I?"

"Zel. Don't be bitter and spiny about it. It won't help."

A breath of frustration—and hurt—whooshed from her lungs. She'd had several days to ponder this. Wrestle with it. At the end of it all, she was left with two things: Bennett wasn't moving on this. And if she wanted his heart back, she was going to have to fight for it.

"I don't want to lose him," she whispered.

"He doesn't want that either." Hunter stepped closer. "That's not why he did what he did."

So Hunter had talked about this with Bennett. Even though she'd asked him not to. Hazel tamped down the rising ire that came with the insecurity of feeling exposed.

One hand pulled from his pocket and covered his shoulder. "Could be a really good thing for you both."

"How was it for you with Janie when she told you she wanted friendship?"

"Hard." He stepped back and folded his arms across his chest. "But my story and your story aren't the same. If you'll think back all those years ago, Janie and I were friends long before we were anything else. And besides, you're tougher than me. Way more stubborn."

At her lifted look, he winked.

Hazel snorted a soft laugh. "Yeah I am."

"Put all that insane stubbornness toward figuring it out with Bennett, hmm?"

She nodded, then allowed a sly grin to poke one side of her mouth upward. She gestured toward the firing range at her side. "This can't hurt, right?"

Hunter leaned back and laughed. "Working through Nathan, you mean?" He shook his head. "Nope. Can't hurt at all."

"You seem tense."

Bennett glanced at his mom, who sat in the passenger seat, and frowned. "You've been saying that on and off for a week."

"Tension isn't good for you."

"That may be true, but sometimes it's a reality of life." He gripped the steering wheel harder as he guided the vehicle past Hazel's cabin and into the final curve to the lodge.

"You prayed about it, right?"

With a glance at the rearview mirror, Bennett saw Gemma watching him and caught Nathan's quick glance. Great. Both kids were listening to this conversation. One he was tired of having. He'd thought that if all of them knew the relationship status between Hazel and himself, they'd let him be. Sulk quietly on his own while he searched for some kind of clarity about how to be now that his hopes had been quashed.

Nope. Mom in particular kept "checking" on him.

"Mom. You know the answer to that because I've told you. Yes. I prayed. I'm still praying. And even though this is the direction I feel God has pushed me to, I'm not a fan of it. So. That leaves me tense, and I can't just make that go away."

With a raised brow, Mom met his glance as he parked the car. Then . . . she smirked. The woman—his own mother!—smirked at his heartache.

What in the world.

Mom patted his arm. "And you used to tell me that Christians lived a delusional life full of easy answers."

The indignation starching his shoulders washed away, leaving him slumped. "I said that?" Once again Bennett was reminded of what a jerk he'd been. How did his mother cling to love when he'd been so awful?

The two kids in the back exchanged a glance and then silently exited, a double *pop, pop* sounding as they shut their doors before trekking to the lodge.

The hand on his arm squeezed. "It takes courage and strength to follow God, no matter what. I'm proud of you, Bennett. And for the record, I know this is hard for both you and Hazel. I'm praying for you."

"Thanks." Bennett again swallowed the swell of emotion. He felt unworthy and desperate. Exhausted and terribly anxious about what this day would hold. It'd been several days since he'd seen Hazel last—and he wasn't sure she'd show up today.

As he gazed at the beautiful log building in front of him and the frozen pond beyond it, Bennett hoped Hazel would come. And was terrified she would.

God, I don't know how to do this... How did he tuck away the deep love he still held for her? How could he build a genuine friendship with a woman who had hurt him and yet he still longed for?

It was a big ask. Much too big for a small, selfish man such as Bennett Crofton.

He turned his attention back to his mom, who watched him with an oddly confident expression. She'd walked some hard paths. Harder, really, than he probably understood. And yet ... yet here she was. A woman whose smile reached her eyes, whose peaceful countenance was unwavering. A woman who had overcome bitterness and anger and embraced forgiveness.

That's the miracle. That had been her claim when he'd asked her how she'd been able to forgive his father. *God's work.*

He closed his eyes. *Work in me.*

"He'll do it," Mom said.

Had she read his mind—heard his silent prayer?

Patting his arm one last time, Mom offered an encouraging smile and then left him alone. Bennett watched as she strode to the side steps of the deck, where Mama B met her. The two women embraced as if they'd been lifelong friends. For the near-instant bond Bennett had observed between the pair, they might as well have been.

And he was thankful for that. Mom deserved all the joy she could find.

Alone in his car, Bennett took a moment to practice some intentional gratitude, thanking God for his mom's unwavering, stubborn love. For providing joy in her life, despite the hard disappointments she'd experienced. And for bringing them all to Luna.

Yes, he was still thankful for that. It'd been a year now since he'd decided to move, and though things hadn't worked out the way he'd hoped, he was glad to be in the middle of this wilderness wonder. With these complicated, amazing people. He wouldn't go back—not unless God told him to.

A flash of movement to his right snagged his attention, and he turned to find Hunter and Hazel emerging from the ridge trail. His heart clenched, as he couldn't help but zero in on the small woman wearing mukluks and a red-plaid, fur-lined trapper's hat. That honied braid hung over her shoulder, contrasting with her dark corduroy coat. By looking at her, one would think nothing had changed. She still owned the loveliest face he'd ever seen. Still rendered him breathless at a mere glimpse.

But everything had changed.

Anxiety spun a reckless knot in his gut as her attention turned his way. She slowed her stride, and Hunter, beside her, looked from Bennett then to her, then leaned in to speak a quick word near her ear. Hunter nodded at Bennett and quickened his stride toward the lodge.

Hazel stopped and waited. For him?

Bennett's heart strummed as he pushed out of the car, shut the door, and met Hazel on the path.

"Hi," she said.

It took way too much self-discipline not to reach for her, to pull her against him and tell her he'd changed his mind. Never mind the friendship he knew they needed to find. Forget his convictions. What he wanted was to be with her.

God, help.

"Hey." His voice came out raspy. He cleared his throat and shoved his gaze toward the pines at her back. "I wasn't sure I'd see you here today."

"Yeah. Well, here I am."

"Hunter?"

"Yeah. He's a pest."

Bennett allowed himself to find her eyes. Blue and beautiful, as always. But guarded. And wounded. His heart squeezed again. *You're going to have to try hard if you want this to work.*

"He just wants you to be a part of his life."

A halfhearted attempt at a smile faltered on her lips. She looked away, and for several moments, nothing but the white puffs of their breath, the gentle stirring of wind through pine boughs, and the swirling shush of snow on the frozen lake existed between them. Then Hazel turned back to him.

"I've been working on a plan for helping Nathan with the biathlon."

"What?"

"Nathan texted me, asking about biathlons—if I knew anything about them and if I could teach him." As she spoke, she seemed both confused by his puzzlement and enthusiastic for this new endeavor.

"I didn't know anything about a biathlon. Nathan didn't mention anything about it to me."

"Oh." Her shoulders fell.

On instinct Bennett reached for her but caught himself before his hand landed on her arm. "That doesn't mean it's a bad idea. I just didn't know. Actually, I don't know anything about biathlons in general."

"It's cross-country skiing and marksmanship."

"As in shooting?"

She swallowed, bracing her stance. "I know you still don't like guns, but this is a skilled event. Competition. It's not like—"

"Hazel."

She stopped, pinning her lips together in a frown.

"I'm not saying no. I'm just clarifying."

"Oh." She nodded. "Okay. I had to read up on it—but for his age group it's a total of 12k skiing, broken into rounds of 3k, with shooting in between each loop. There's a 150-meter penalty loop for every missed shot."

"And it's a race?"

"Yes."

"And Nathan wants to try it?"

"That's what it sounded like. He asked if I could teach him."

Bennett took this news in while he rubbed his bearded jaw.

"Bennett, I know how to ski, and I'm a good shot. It's sort of my jam, if you remember."

He chuckled. "I remember."

Nathan doing something that didn't involve a screen? Bennett would jump at that for that reason alone. Something that would involve Hazel, requiring her to stay in his orbit? Even better.

"I think this could be good for him. Something completely different than anything he's ever tried. And the fact that he's interested in it at all is—"

"Zel." This time Bennett didn't resist the urge to reach out and touch her. "I'm not saying no. In fact, I agree with you. It might be really good for him. I'm surprised, is all. Like I said, he didn't mention it to me. And you—"

Her gaze clamped on to his and held. Some of the guardedness melted away as those blue eyes warmed.

"Are you sure you're up for it?" Bennett asked.

"I am." Hazel bit her bottom lip. "I think it might be fun."

She was excited about this too! "Okay."

"Okay? As in yes?"

Bennett chuckled. "Yes."

She swallowed, her stare unmoving but fading back into that caution. "You'll have to bring him up here for it."

And see her. "I understand that." It would be a welcome opportunity to work on this friendship, even if it was hard.

"And I might ... We might need your help sometimes."

"I would like that."

"Yeah?"

"Yeah, Hazel." Old habits pressed, and Bennett had to bat back the instinct to lace his fingers with hers. "I would very much like to be a part of it."

Hazel ducked her face, obscuring his view of her emotions. For a handful of breaths, they fell into awkward, tension-filled silence. Then she squared her shoulders and nodded at him. "Good. We'll start as soon as your mom clears him for full activity."

"Sounds good. Mom told me this week he's about done with physical therapy." A surprising touch of mild amusement tickled Bennett. Her all-business, matter-of-fact demeanor reminded him of the first day they'd met, when she'd informed him that she was not taking him up to the cabin because he wasn't likely to survive. What a spitfire she'd been that day.

Hazel started toward the lodge. Bennett reached for her again and smiled when she met his eyes. "Thank you, Zel."

Ah, there in that soft look was that tenderness he longed for. But careful, careful ... Bennett leaned back, tucking his hands back into his coat pockets.

"You're welcome, Bennett." For a brief moment her fingers brushed his arm. Then she offered a tempered smile before she continued toward the lodge.

Bennett's heart swelled with love. Maybe he wasn't supposed to tuck it away completely?

Maybe he was supposed to learn how to love differently.

CHAPTER ELEVEN

"THIS IS LIVY." NERVES bit into Janie's stomach as she presented the girl to Bennett and the kids. Did she dare introduce her as her sister? Of all people, Bennett would get it—the internal flailing Janie had going on about her newly discovered half sibling. Then again, he'd taken his siblings in and was doing remarkably with it all. So maybe it was just Janie who bubbled around, pinging between guilt, resentment, awkwardness, and a sense of obligation.

There was the little detail, however, of Bennett having known about his half siblings, where this was all brand-new news to Janie. Did that give her a pass?

With a quick glance toward Mama, her decision was made. "She's staying with me for a few days."

She felt, more than saw, Hunter's mild disapproval and had no doubt he wore a scowl. Livy tossed her a raised-brow glance. She had been with them for a few days now, and Janie still hadn't told Mama about the situation. At least, not all of it.

Hunter hadn't been on that page with Janie. Livy had said she didn't care either way. By that sharp look, she did though.

"It's good to meet you, Livy." Mama stretched out a hand and grasped Livy by the elbow, giving her a kind squeeze. "Janie mentioned she had a guest staying with her." Mama's eyes wandered toward Janie. "I'm not sure why she hasn't brought you across the road to introduce you already."

Janie choked down a cough. Reasons. That was why.

How was Janie supposed to tell her mother that her ex-husband's secret kid had found her way into their lives, though? She wasn't sure she possessed that sort of delicacy, and she was certain she didn't own the fortitude.

She painted on a smile and aimed it at her mother, even while the first time she'd mentioned Livy to Mama plunked through her mind.

"She's on a little adventure—maybe a bit misguided," Janie had told Mama, with Hunter standing right there to witness her half-truth. At his throat clearing, Janie had shot him a hushing frown, then returned to Mama's curious watch. "Hunter and I are deciding if we should give her money to get back home or take her down to Austin ourselves."

Mama had arched an eyebrow as she met Janie's false cheer. Like she knew something was up.

Of course Mama knew something was up. Along with lacking delicacy and fortitude, Janie was not endowed with the ability to act. At least not convincingly.

Did Mama know . . . about Livy?

The suspicious possibility flared a spark of resentment. If Mama had known all along . . .

A large hand spread against her back, and then Hunter's warmth enveloped her from the side. "What do you say we get some paint on these walls?"

Standing near the stone fireplace, Gemma bounced on her toes and clapped. "Now we're talking. I have experience with this. Let me at it."

"Right. You've painted one room, and you had to have four people help you. You're exaggerating." Nathan eyed his sister and shook his head. "As usual."

"Keep your grumpy attitude on lockdown, Nate." Gemma cast a sour expression toward Nathan and then walked toward Livy. "We'll have the best time, right?"

Livy met Gemma's enthusiasm with an expressionless look. After a beat too long, she shrugged. "Sure."

Gemma's high-energy brightness flickered, and her eyes held mild defeat as she looked at Janie.

"We'll make it beautiful in here." Janie stepped out of Hunter's light touch and tucked Gemma under one arm. Then she reached and wrapped her free arm around Livy. "Let's make the Splendor's guest rooms glorious."

"The paint and all the supplies are in the kitchen." Hunter motioned toward the back of the lodge as he referenced the haul he and Janie had purchased when they'd made a shopping expedition to Bozeman after Christmas. Paint, wallpaper, supplies, and a few decorations that Janie had loved had all made their way back to the lodge with them.

Warmth pooled in Janie's belly as she thought back on that day. Hunter had surprised her with a real date. He'd arranged for Tara to take the café for the day, taken Janie out to eat, and then, when they'd gone shopping, he'd kissed her mouth and told her to make the Splendor stunning.

Their home. Well, more like their business venture, as they'd technically be living in the carriage house. But it was sort of the same.

She allowed her gaze to wander, traveling from that impressive fireplace, over the gleaming wood floors, around the massive front room, up to the vaulted ceiling, and then over to the wide staircase.

Wow. Just . . . wow. This was theirs.

Well, it was Hunter's at the moment. But it was going to be *theirs*, just as soon as May would hurry up and get there.

The trio of girls trailed behind Hunter as he led the way to the decor loot in the kitchen. Behind them came Mama and Tara, exchanging a soft conversation about the cleanup process happening at the old Tellings Hardware store.

Bennett, Hazel, and Nathan stayed in the great room, in the middle of what seemed to be a great silence. Yikes. Friendship seemed like a good idea for Bennett and Hazel. Good and awful at the same time, because she knew exactly how hard it had been to do between herself and Hunter.

Actually. Hunter had tried. He really had, and it hadn't been a total failure. Hadn't he stayed at the café to finish her cleaning up job so she could go hiking with Grady? Hadn't he tried to call off the stupid bet made in a highly emotional moment? And hadn't he texted her his encouragement even when she was out on a backpacking trip with another guy?

Hunter had tried to be her friend. And even though it didn't always work out well for him, and even though jealousy and frustration had gotten the upper hand on his intentions on a few occasions, his efforts had mattered. In fact, without them Janie might not have realized her own failures in their relationship. And without his attempts at friendship, she wouldn't have allowed the longing for more to be set free.

Maybe friendship was exactly what Bennett and Hazel needed right now.

"Wow." Mama stepped ahead of Janie as she examined the load of wedding decorations crowding the empty pantry in the corner of the kitchen. "Did you clean Hobby Lobby out?"

"Basically." Hunter grinned, as if this were an accomplishment.

Tara laughed. "Must be a groom-to-be." She turned to Janie and winked. "Take advantage of it while you can, my dear."

Janie shook her head. Truth was, Hunter was excessively generous and always had been. The stingy Wallace was still back in the great room. Casting out her great silence.

"This doesn't look unusual for Hunt," Mama said. "Not when it comes to my Janie. He'd buy the moon and name it after her if he could." She turned and looked at Janie. "Janie, however, is not usually this extravagant."

Guilt nipped at her heart. Mama was right—this was extravagant, and Janie was usually more level headed. Business required it. But with Hunter . . .

He had a way of making her lose her sensibilities. In good ways and bad.

"Some of that is only for the wedding." She pointed out three bags of greenery. "But most of it will useful year round for other things. And the lights—we'll use them again for any other events this magnificent lodge hosts, and Lord willing, that will be more than a few."

"Touché." Mama winked and then gave Janie a side hug. "I should have known you wouldn't be impulsive." Mischief edged her teasing grin. "Even if you did get engaged two weeks after you started dating."

Livy's chin jerked around from the large bag of white glittery floral picks—all of which would also be reused for the wedding. "Two weeks?" Those blue eyes were wide with astonishment.

"It was the most romantic thing you've ever saw." Gemma swooned.

"That's not the full story."

Livy's right eyebrow arched. "Sounds like you're more like Dad than you think."

Every eye in the room turned and landed first on Livy and then quickly shot to Janie. The air in the room froze. No one moved. No one breathed.

Janie's pulse slugged hard and slow, her blood a sludgy mix of fire and ice. She swallowed as she inched her wide-eyed stare from Livy to Mama.

Mama pinned her lips closed and kept a cool gaze on Janie.

"I think we'd better take these paint buckets outside and get them stirred up well and good." Tara lifted a pail and handed it to Gemma, who stood gaping.

"They mix them at the store," Gemma muttered, not taking her gaze from the trio of women at the center of attention. "I'm sure they're fine."

Hunter cleared his throat. "No, Tara is right. Paint settles. You have to make sure you get the consistency and color right again." He took up two more pails and nudged Gemma toward the door.

Livy bit her bottom lip, glanced from Janie to Mama and back again, then skedaddled after Hunter, Tara, and Gemma. "Hand me a stick and a bucket of paint."

The heavy swinging wood door whapped once, twice, and then a third and final time as the onlookers made their escape. Then it was just Janie and Mama.

Janie mashed her lips together and tried, unsuccessfully, to lift her gaze off the floor to meet her mother's unwavering watch. She swallowed—which was more of a gulp, as the lump swelling in her throat made it difficult.

"Janie Elizabeth."

Two names and a tone that demanded eye contact. Not. Good.

She swallowed—gulped—again. "Mama, I know this is a shock, but—"

"That you lied to me? Yes. That is a shock."

"I didn't lie."

"Nowhere in your hurried, odd explanation about why Hunter was staying with me and why you had a teenage girl staying with you did you mention that she was your sister."

"I was working on that."

"You were lying to me about it."

"I didn't want you to be upset."

"Upset?" Mama scowled. "You think I'm upset because your dad fathered another daughter and the girl came here because she wanted to meet you? Give me some credit here, Janie. Your dad and I divorced. He moved on—which frankly happened long before he left. It happens—a whole lot more than most people want to admit. And it was a long time ago—I've worked through it."

"But clearly you're upset!"

Mama crossed her arms. "I'm upset because you didn't tell me the truth. And because you didn't tell me the truth, you made everyone here uncomfortable."

Janie lowered her face as she blinked. She didn't know what to say—she'd been trying to protect Mama. Could she understand that?

"Janie."

With a sigh, Janie summoned an apology—one she didn't truly feel.

Mama didn't wait for Janie's forced words. "I can certainly be kind to a high school kid who is a little bit turned around, no matter who her dad is. I think the real issue here is that you aren't comfortable with it."

"Of course I'm not. Why would I be? Dad left, and I remember how you were when he did. Now I find out he went off and made a new family. One he stayed with. Did he never look back? Did he never wonder about us? About me? Where does that leave me, Mama?"

Mama's challenging gaze softened, and she nodded. Closing the gap between them, she reached out a strong hand to hold Janie's shoulder. "I think it leaves you with a clear realization that you haven't forgiven him."

Janie winced. That wasn't what this was about. This was about . . .

What then?

Sometimes truth came with a stinging bite.

"My dear daughter." Mama closed in, wrapping her arm around Janie's shoulders. "That is a tough thing to wrestle with, and I'm going to be praying for you because it's time you deal with it. But in the meantime, you've got to square with the fact that none of that is Livy's fault. You can't hold your dad against her."

"I'm n—" Janie swallowed back the lie. Because yeah, she was. She'd muscled up enough do-the-right-thing grit to take Olivia in, but not really. Not into her heart.

Not as a sister.

Mama squeezed. "We'll do it together, hmm?"

"You can?" This still seemed unbelievable to Janie. Why didn't this cut Mama the way it cut her?

"She's a tender soul out searching for something to make her heart whole." Mama let her arms slide off Janie's shoulders and stepped back. "That sort always, ever needs one thing."

"Jesus," Janie whispered.

"He literally brought her to your doorstep, Janie. You didn't even have to *go* anywhere." Mama nodded. "That puts you on mission."

"Is that—" Suddenly Mama's heart made more sense. "Is that why you took Hunter and Hazel in?"

"At the root of it? Yes. God showed me their need—physical and spiritual. And boy, do I love them." Mama's shoulders slipped a little. "I just keep hoping they see more than a woman who wanted to help. I keep hoping they see Jesus."

Hunter did. It had just taken him a while to understand what he saw. And Hazel . . . she saw something—she just didn't get it. Yet. And Janie? Janie always thought her mama's heart was larger than life. It sort of made her feel intimidated, to be honest. How could she ever live up to her mama's giant love?

Janie reached to grasp Mama's hand. "They do, Mama. We all do."

But maybe that big love wasn't Mama's after all? Not entirely, anyway. It was fueled by the love giver Himself.

What a way to live.

CHAPTER TWELVE

HAZEL HADN'T EVER BEEN much good at aesthetics. Function regardless of form was her way of life.

Odd. She savored the rich beauty of nature. It never failed to put her in awe.

That contradiction stirred up all kinds of queries for which Hazel didn't have answers. She wasn't too keen to steep in the discomfort of deeper implications as she helped smooth a rich buttercream paint on the walls. With a hard mental shove, she banished the questions concerning nature and awe and the wonderings that were becoming more common and insistent from the forefront of her thoughts.

"When can we start?" Nathan's question aided Hazel's shift in mindset, voiced from the opposite side of the wall they were painting.

She knew exactly what he was talking about. It was weird and exciting that he was so focused on this biathlon thing.

"Whenever you want." Hazel grinned. "But we have to clear a course first, and you're going to be in on that work."

Nathan didn't flinch. Another good anomaly. "Can we walk it today?"

Hazel glanced at Bennett, his roller coloring the opposite wall on the other side of the large guest suite.

He nodded. "I don't see why not—as long as we aren't needed here."

"It's a good day for it," Hazel said. "Sunshine but not too warm, so the snow won't be slush."

"Can we try the skis?" Nathan asked. "I've never done the cross-country kind and only have tried downhill twice."

Hazel shook her head. "Not yet. We should do your first run on an established trail with a little less elevation change. Like the one at Elk Creek in town. I know of several people who ski the upper section regularly, so it should be packed and good to go."

"When can we do that?"

Bennett chuckled. "What brought this on, Nathan?"

Nathan glared at Bennett, no doubt irritated to be laughed at. Feeling defensive for the kid, and a little put out that Bennett tamped his enthusiasm, Hazel shot the older of the two a scowl.

Bennett bent to place his roller in the pan. "I think it's great, buddy."

"Me too," Hazel said.

Nathan loaded his roller with more paint and faced the wall again.

"I was just curious how you even thought about a biathlon." Bennett crossed the space and clapped a hand on Nathan's shoulder. "It's not common, you know?"

Nathan's pinched brow relaxed, and then he looked . . . embarrassed? He shrugged Bennett's hand away and moved over to work on an untouched section of the wall. "Nothing really. I just . . . heard about it at school. It sounded cool. Different. Not like the regular jock stuff."

Jock stuff . . . Nathan spit that out with a strong taste of resentment.

"Not like Dad's football stories?" Bennett said.

Nathan shrugged. "Whatever. I don't really care what Dad did or didn't do. Or what he does now, for that matter."

Not one bit of that was true. Hazel would bet on it. That was like her saying that she hadn't cared what Hunter had done when he'd left Elk Lake. She'd cared deeply—that was why she'd been so blazing mad at him for it.

Nathan turned back to the paint pan to reload. "I thought you'd be for it, since you're always telling me to do something that requires more movement than just my thumbs. And besides, if I'm gonna be stuck here, I might as well do something I wouldn't be able to do back in Chicago."

Hazel caught Bennett's glance over the top of Nathan's black slouch beanie—a look that said he wasn't buying Nathan's cavalier attitude about their dad either, but he wasn't going to chase down the lie.

Bennett nudged Nathan and waited for him to straighten. "Like I said, I think it's great. We're lucky to have Hazel. I can't imagine anyone better to teach you how to shoot straight, and I wouldn't even know where to begin with the skiing part."

Hazel's chest warmed at Bennett' s words. Even with everything strained and awkward between them, he'd been kind. What kind of man had she rejected?

What kind of fool did that make her?

A lost one.

There was that voice again—the one that had kept asking all those pesky questions, probing at the emptiness she'd just as soon deny was there all together.

She heaved another mental shove. "We'll start at the shooting range behind my cabin, walk the trapline trail, then cut across the ridge and make a big circle around the pond and the lake. That should give us the distance we need, but we'll take my GPS just to be certain."

"Good." Nathan smacked his hands together and moved toward the door. "I've had about all I can take of painting, and this unending wedding playlist is getting on my nerves."

"Hold up." Bennett put up a hand. "Let me run it by Hunter and make sure we're not needed with anything else—*after* we finish this room."

"Man, how much more could there be? Pretty sure we could have painted our Chicago house twice by now."

With a sweeping examination of the room, Hazel had to agree. They'd been at this for a few hours, and the whole time, a nonstop string of love songs had been their backdrop. The first round of the sappy music had been fine. Ish. She'd blocked out the fact that the man she loved but was no longer with was working in the same space as her. Round two of the mushy music had been more than enough. Take three . . . Oy.

She peeked at Bennett, heat climbing her neck. Did the music tug painfully at him the way she wished it didn't her?

"This lodge is a little bigger than your house," Bennett said, rescuing Hazel from the painful ruminating.

Nathan shrugged. "A little."

That didn't seem to be sarcastic. Hazel was reminded of the wealth Bennett had at his back, and she wondered with a gnawing worry if he'd ever wish to go back to it. Back to the city, back to the luxury condos, the expensive restaurants, the tailored suits . . . and all the *perks* that had gone with his former life.

He proposed. You were the one to say no. That silent reminder did little to settle her anxiety. After all, they weren't even dating now. What really held Bennett Crofton to Luna? To her?

Nothing. Nothing more than this uneasy attempt at a friendship that she had no navigation for, and his declaration that he'd always love her.

Did love endure through this?

"There!" Gemma's triumphant call came from somewhere down the hall. "It's glorious!"

Janie's soft laugh followed Gemma's exuberance. "It does look good."

"Then we're done, right?" Livy sounded less thrilled and more exhausted than the other two.

"We must inspect every inch before we can make that sort of finalizing declaration. No white splotches on the walls—after all, this is the *honeymoon* suite."

"Gemma, you're always over the top." Nathan crossed his arms. "Enough already."

From the wide hallway separating the two guest suites, Gemma poked her head into their workspace and stuck out her tongue. "Did it hurt your tiny, cold heart to listen to love songs all day?"

"Yes."

"You're never going to get a girlfriend. You do realize that, right?"

Nathan winced and looked toward the floor. Had that jab actually landed somewhere tender?

"Time out, Croftons." Janie held out both hands, as if keeping the siblings from literally going at it. "I think it's time to get that lasagna into the oven. Hungry bellies make for grumpy helpers."

"I am never grumpy," Gemma crossed her arms and aimed a raised-brow look at Nathan.

"You're never normal either." Nathan flicked the ball cap Gemma had borrowed from Bennett off her head, then looked at Janie. "I could go for food."

"I'm not normal?" Gemma recovered her hat. "You're one to talk."

"Are you two always like this?" Livy asked.

"Gemma is always ridiculous." Nathan stalked down the hall toward the wide staircase. "And self-righteous."

"Nathan is always lame." Gemma put on a sugary smile as she called after him. "But I love him anyway."

Nathan whipped out his phone as he clomped down the steps.

Hazel looked at Bennett just in time to see him cover his eyes with one hand to rub his temples. They all needed a break.

"We could go walk around the lakes," Hazel said to Bennett, keeping the suggestion between them. "Get at least that measurement before dinner."

"Good idea." Bennett lifted one corner of his mouth in an attempt at a smile. "Maybe Nathan will shake off this sudden sour mood."

"He's been doing pretty well up until now." And she could hardly blame him for wilting. She needed outside too. Maybe more than the kid.

Bennett let a long breath out slowly. "Yeah." This time he did manage a full smile. "Yeah, he has. And Gemma is just trying to overcome the awkwardness from earlier today. Trying to take the attention off Janie."

The urge to step nearer and rub his tense back nearly overtook her sense of reality. That was what she would have done before, when they were dating.

Did friends do such things? Hazel had no idea. She'd had exactly one true friend in her life, and that had been Janie, who was more like a sister than the sort of friend Bennett had asked Hazel to be.

She didn't have long to ponder it. Bennett reached across the space between them, his hand landing on her shoulder. He gave her a gentle squeeze and then let his touch fall away. "Thanks, Zel."

With that, he turned and walked toward Hunter.

Apparently that was how this friendship thing worked. Kindness—enough to make her wish to have back the loving looks that had previously come with it. Touch—the sort that was distant and too short, making her long for the lingering warmth of his fingers.

Could she really do this?

The wounded part of her wanted to yell *no*. To march herself back to her cabin and lock herself away. To be alone to tend her sore heart and sulk. She'd go back to her life of isolation. One she'd been perfectly content with before.

But the other part—the one that wanted desperately *not* to lose everything she'd had with Bennett—knew better. And chose to do better. Because she couldn't go back to contented isolation. She couldn't name why exactly, but she knew progress was possible.

Tucking away the little girl who had wanted to storm away and pout, Hazel watched while Bennett and her brother exchanged a few words. Hunter looked interested, and when he shifted his attention to Hazel, he looked pleased. Proud, even. Then he nodded, and both men made a path toward the stairs. Hazel followed after them, and they found Nathan leaning against the fireplace.

"We're on." Bennett elbowed Nathan.

Nathan jerked his head up from his phone. "Yeah?"

"I'm a little jealous," Hunter said. "If I didn't have three other things to juggle right now, I'd be in on this too. Isn't the little Harmond girl into biathlons?"

Lips pinned tight and cheeks warming to a suspicious pink, Nathan ducked his head and headed toward the door and walked outside. Huh. Suddenly Nathan's reaction to Gemma's reference to a *girlfriend* made a little more sense.

Bennett's brows lifted. "The little Harmond girl . . . who would that be?"

"Ella Harmond." Hunter looked at Hazel. "Remember her? She used to come into the Pantry with her kitten. She'd tell Mama B that she couldn't leave the thing outside because it would feel 'abandoned' and that would be too sad. She was cute."

"How old is she?"

"Now?" Hunter paused, doing a mental calculation, then looked back at Hazel. "Fifteen? Sixteen?"

Hazel shrugged, keeping one eye on Bennett. "I don't know. I remember her, but only because of the kitten. I haven't kept track of her."

"So you don't know if she's pretty or what she's like," Bennett said.

Hazel shrugged. Why would she know that? "Janie would be the better one to ask. She knows everyone." She held a warning stare on Bennett. "Might be better to just let that one lie though."

Amusement made those blue eyes twinkle, but Bennett nodded.

Nathan's limp was almost nonexistent. Bennett swelled with relief. Hopefully, Mom would clear him for full activity this week, and they could get started with this newest activity. It was good to see Nathan interested in something other than a screen. And noteworthy to discover that it'd been a girl who had provoked it.

Hazel had warned him to let that one alone. She got Nathan. Better than Bennet did, and wasn't that a flip of the script? So he had agreed to leave the question of Ella Hammond alone. For now.

Curiosity about it stirred though, and as he trailed behind Hazel and Nathan, he plotted how and when he'd get to meet this girl. Maybe she'd come up with them to train sometime? Would a competitor offer her experience to someone who might become her rival on the course? Would Nathan feel embarrassed or annoyed to have a girl he liked be better than him?

Bennett hoped not. And he hoped this Ella was a sweet kid who would be nice to Nathan. One who would draw out a kindness and manliness from a boy who had been pretty self-absorbed and snarky.

Someone like Hazel had been for the former Bennett Crofton.

His attention zeroed in on the woman blazing their trail. A half smile teased his mouth as she pointed out a new meter mark, and then she and Nathan discussed something. Bennett had half expected that she wouldn't show up at the lodge to paint today.

Well, more than half. The Hazel he'd first met would have nailed her door shut and hibernated until June, refusing to see anyone, just to spite him for making her mad. He'd sort of guessed she'd revert to that badger-lady personality.

Is that really what he thought of the woman he loved?

Shame and ache pinned deep in his chest. Love hoped for all things—good things. Believed. And he did love her. It was the certainty of that love that kept him there.

But this? Hazel there, trying the way she was? Not just with Nathan—she was trying with *him*. Fighting for a friendship even though he knew it wasn't what she wanted. Seemed she'd changed—grown as much as Bennett had. Perhaps they were good for each other after all.

It was an uplifting surprise.

Restored hope eased the pain and lent some peace. Maybe finding friendship in the midst of their convoluted relationship wouldn't be as hard as he'd expected.

Maybe they were right where they needed to be.

CHAPTER
THIRTEEN

HAZEL TUCKED ANOTHER PINE log into the woodburning stove and closed the glass door. Orange flames bounced light into the dimming cabin, its cheer warming her as much as the building heat. Remaining in her crouched position, she tucked her grandmother's sweater tighter around her shoulders and breathed in the pungent aroma of burning wood.

It'd been a good day. A surprisingly good day.

She tucked her chin against her shoulder and smiled. Nathan's enthusiasm for this biathlon thing hadn't waned, even when the walk around the lakes turned chilly and they'd found a spot that would take some muscle and sweat to clear.

And Bennett . . .

He'd gripped her hand at the end of the evening, when their tummies were full of Janie's lasagna and their bodies were sufficiently tired from a day of decorating and adventure. Those familiar fingers—now rough from chopping firewood and building his own fires and becoming a mountain man rather than a city boy—had squeezed hers briefly.

"Thanks, Zel. This means a lot." He'd removed his touch and turned to join the kids at the car but then paused and let those gorgeous blue eyes linger on hers. "To both me and Nathan."

Perhaps this friendship wasn't impossible.

The impression of his warm hands rushed back. Suddenly the room felt cozy. She'd never be satisfied with *just friends* with that man. But for the time—and with the hope for more again someday—his tender friendship was sweet. It was certainly a whole lot better than the hollow sensation of loss that had consumed her when she'd believed he was done with her entirely. Maybe even better than the angsty and somewhat volatile romance they'd found themselves in over the past several months.

Caught off guard by that realization, Hazel latched tight the door to the stove and stood. She walked to the window overlooking the lake and watched the colors of the sunset fade to gray and then quickly melt into velvet black. The clouds had cleared, allowing the stars to reach Elk Canyon with vibrant light, each white sparkle distinct and stunning.

Hazel grabbed her coat and walked out the front door—a nightly habit. Her feet found the familiar trail to the dock. Bending over an Adirondack chair, she dusted off the light coating of snow from earlier that day and sat exactly where she'd spent hundreds of evenings before. As the moonless sky darkened, the silent beauty of the night swathed her heart with its familiar wonder.

Love felt like this. Big and thrilling. Beautiful and awesome. Unfathomable and yet inescapable. And intimidating.

Her arms prickled with that thought, but oddly her mind shifted from Bennett to something . . . undefined. It whispered in a language she couldn't distinguish, imprinting on her heart. Her soul.

Hazel stared at the wonder above her. Surrounding her. It called, but without words. It sang, the melody a haunting thrill in her soul.

"Who are you?" she whispered.

Wonder filled her being, and Hazel didn't blink. She didn't want to miss the beauty. The mystery. As the wonder grew, so did longing. Who sang this lingering serenade to her soul? What were the words? And was it a love song for her?

Who would compose such a masterpiece for a snarky mountain girl like her?

This woman she now was—she wasn't familiar. Hazel examined the stranger she'd become—one with more tenderness, more kindness—and wondered if she liked her. She was infinitely more vulnerable, and that was scary. But also more likable, if her budding connection with Nathan and her better relationship with Hunter were any indication. Was the trade-off worth it?

Hazel didn't have a definite answer. But that didn't stop a new question from burgeoning.

Was this softening due to Bennett?

Yes.

No?

Maybe some?

What was going on with her? This . . . this *awakening*—did a man have the power to rouse a woman's soul from the dead? To summon life where there had been a cold grave, to unstop deaf ears so she could hear the symphony of the cosmos?

Did Bennett wield that sort of magic?

She stared at the sky, let the silent music of the stars disturb her waking heart. *Not Bennett. Not all Bennett.*

With that clear whisper, a memory reached from her distant past. A melody from her childhood, the lyrics startlingly clear.

Lord, how your wonders are displayed,
where'er we turn our eyes,
if we survey the ground we tread
or gaze upon the skies.

That was Nan's voice, steady and pure, singing. What was the song?

Hazel blinked, startled to find moisture lining the skin beneath her eyes. Though she *felt* more than she *thought*, confusion swirled through her. Countless times she'd sat beneath starry night skies. Appreciated the beauty of the unpolluted view from her lake. Had even savored the awesomeness of its immensity.

But never like this. Never with her soul cracking wide open.

What had just happened?

Hunter shut off the large overhead light in the vaulted entry area of the great room. The quiet night outside blended into the lodge, soft black gently illuminated by the muted yellow twinkle lights encircling the stair banisters, along with a eucalyptus garland. Janie hadn't been able to resist putting it up. At the center of each window, and on each riser of that wide staircase, the flicker of electronic candles held by oversized hurricane lanterns added to the romantic ambiance.

Janie sure had some impressive vision. He couldn't wait to see all that she would do for their wedding.

The woman at his side slipped an arm around him. Hunter soaked in the warm sense of contentment and joy as he tucked Janie in close and pressed a kiss to her head. "It's stunning, love."

She giggled softly. "It is quite beautiful, isn't it?"

"Everything you hoped it would be, I would think. It's sure taking my breath away."

"Hmm. We're not done yet." She snuggled in deeper and then sighed. This time her satisfaction seemed tainted.

"It isn't what you envisioned?" Hunter leaned back to catch a glimpse of her face in the soft light.

"It's beautiful. I'm happy." She raised up on her toes and pecked his cheek. "Thank you for making it possible."

"Something seems wrong."

"It's just that the day started sideways. That was a little disappointing, and it's still nagging me."

Hunter moved to lay a gentle hold on her shoulders. "Janie, it went well. There was one little blip, but everyone moved on."

She crossed her arms and rubbed them. "I wish Livy hadn't done that."

"It was bound to come out sometime. Everyone was just surprised, that's all. Especially since you didn't just lead with it in the first place."

"Mama was upset."

"Janie." He tucked a strand of dark hair behind her ear and stooped to gain her eye contact. "MB is as stout as she is kind. She was fine."

"No. She wasn't." Lifting her chin, Janie pinned a firm glare on him, daring him to counter what she knew about her mother.

He knew Mama Bulldog about as well as Janie—after all, he'd been practically raised by the woman too. "She was upset. At you."

Janie blinked. "That's not—"

"Janie Truitt." He shook his head.

Her shoulders slumped. "Okay. Fine. She was upset at me. But I just wanted to protect her. At least until after I figure out what to do."

"What to do about what?"

"How to tell her, I mean."

"Mama B?" He chuckled. "Well, it's done. Maybe you should thank Livy when we pick her up from Bennett's later tonight."

Janie's unimpressed smirk let him know she wasn't going to laugh this off so easily. "This can't be easy for Mama. That's what I'm trying to say. Now we have this shadow again. I'm so tired of shadows."

"Honey, you've got to stop this." Hunter placed his hands on her upper arms. "First, everything isn't going to be perfect. Life just doesn't roll that way. And more importantly, you've got to be honest, even when it's hard." He lowered his voice to a soft plea. "Trust the people who love you to work through those hard things with you."

Irritation pressed lines into Janie's forehead. "Are we talking about Mama and Livy now, or are we revisiting the past?"

Hunter kept his expression placid, refusing the bait for a bad trip down memory lane. Rather than responding, he simply held his place.

After several heartbeats, Janie sighed, lowering her gaze, which had lost its fire. "I'm sorry."

He nudged her close, and she pressed her forehead into his chest. He held her, both arms snug around her, and pressed another kiss into her hair. "MB has one of the biggest hearts I've ever seen, and I'm sure grateful for that. Where would me and Hazel be without her generous love?"

Janie's arms snaked around him. "I know, but that was different."

"I doubt she'll think so. We were two lost, broken kids who needed a kind heart for a home. Not much different from Livy. MB has a special gift for that sort."

"You don't think it will be a challenge to accept that the man she'd married went off and had another family?" Janie stepped back and crossed her arms, her scowl firmly fixed again. "Hunter, I remember when he left. I remember what she looked like when she told me he wasn't coming back."

Hunter reached across the space she'd put between them and fingered her jawline. "I'm not saying it wasn't hard. That's not at all what I think. But I suspect your mom worked through the possibility that your dad moved on—started another life with someone else—a long time ago. She didn't seem all that shocked to hear it from Livy. It seemed more like she was annoyed that you weren't forthright with her." He nudged Janie's chin so that she'd meet his gaze again. "Is it possible that what's really going on here is that *you're* having a hard time accepting that your dad had another family?"

Janie's expression crumbled. When she blinked, a tear seeped down her nose. "He never looked back, Hunt. I never heard from him." She sniffed and wiped at the streak of wetness. "That was bad enough, but I thought he didn't want a family. He wanted to be free. To live his own adventures, no responsibilities holding him back. Now I find out he just didn't want us. Didn't want me." Her voice broke on that last sentence.

Hunter pulled her against him again, holding tight while her shoulders trembled and her tears dampened his shirtfront. A concoction of pity for her wounded heart and anger at her lousy dad made for a powerful mix of emotions.

God, what do we do with this?

Even as he prayed, he allowed this moment to brand his heart. He didn't want to forget how this wrecked Janie. He didn't ever want to be the man to destroy her world—or that of the children they hoped for. He couldn't be the man her father had been.

Unexpectedly, a sequence of scenes flashed through his mind—that of him shutting Hazel in that tack room, of her holding him in contempt for it for years, and then of their reconciliation. Initially, the intrusion didn't make sense.

But.

But then it did.

"There are two sides to every story," he murmured.

"What?" Janie leaned back, the word a breathless ache.

"You don't know your dad's story, hon." Hunter swallowed, knowing this was a tenuous path. He wasn't searching for excuses for Mike Truitt. Honest. But he was all too aware that sometimes actions that looked cruel and selfish weren't intended that way.

There *were* two sides to every story.

"Truthfully, you don't even know Livy's."

Her brow folded into a hard scowl. "What are you trying to say?"

With one hand he cupped her face and smoothed his thumb against the lines carving her forehead. "Nothing you should be mad at me about." He leaned down and kissed the spot above her nose. "Don't tuck that beautiful heart away, Janie. Keep it soft. Like that verse in the book of James talks about—quick to listen, slow to speak, slow to become angry."

For a moment she maintained a glare. But then her shoulders lost their iron and she nodded. Closing the gap that had spread between them, she slipped her arms around him again.

Hunter was only too glad to hold her.

"How is it that you know the Bible like that and you've only recently became a Christian?"

Hunter shrugged, tracing light circles against her back with his fingertips. "John says it's important to know what God wants our lives to be like. That was one of the verses he sent me when something was gnawing at me."

"About me?"

He chuckled. Yeah, it'd been about her—some time between when he'd told her their stupid bet was off and she'd gone through with it anyway.

Worst week and a half of his life.

Janie propped her chin on his chest. "What else do you tell John about me?"

"That you're the love of my life."

Her soft smile warmed those sweet blue eyes, making him mush. "You'll walk with me through this?"

"Every step, babe. I promise." He sealed that vow with a kiss.

CHAPTER FOURTEEN

"I NEED HELP." LIVY's soft voice pulled Janie's attention from the dough she was kneading against the steel counter.

With the heels of her palms deep in the soft, warm cinnamon roll dough, she looked over her shoulder at the girl with her hands deep in dish soap suds. "Sounds serious."

Livy's shoulders drooped, and she hesitated before she looked at Janie. When she did, it was with her bottom lip tucked under her teeth. "I . . . I lied to you. About my mom."

"What?"

Livy's shoulders caved as her face cast toward the floor. "She's not like Dad. She's stable and works really hard. And she just found out that I'm not on that youth ski trip."

"Livy! Why would you lie about that?"

"Because I figured if you thought both of my parents were . . . you know . . ."

"Alcoholics?"

"Yeah. If you thought that, you wouldn't send me home right away." Her hands hung low at her sides, dripping sudsy water onto the tile floor. She peeked up, miserable guilt scrawled across her face. "I just wanted to spend some time with you. Get to know you."

"That's not a good excuse to lie to your mother—or to me." Janie wiped her forehead with the back of her hand and then propped both hands on her hips. "She must be *frantic*, Liv! I can't imagine finding out my daughter took a cross-country trip into the mountains, in the winter, completely alone."

One giant tear welled up and dripped from her eye. "I didn't think she'd worry if she thought—"

"You have to stop making excuses." Janie crossed her arms. Then she sighed. "And we have to get you home."

Livy nodded. "I massively underestimated how much this trip was going to cost. I really do only have the thirty-some dollars left."

Janie nodded. Even if Livy had the money to get herself home, Janie wasn't about to send her newly discovered little sister on the road by herself. "Hunter and I have been talking about how to get you back to Texas."

"You didn't want me here?"

"No, that's not what I said and not why we've been discussing it. You can't just disappear from your life, Liv. You can't just ditch people who care about you." Lowering her arms, Janie stepped across the kitchen and gripped Livy's shoulder. "And it sounds like your mom cares about you."

Livy's chin wobbled as she nodded. "I didn't mean to upset her."

"You should have told her the truth—that you wanted to know who your sister was." Conviction pierced her own heart as she spoke. She'd yet to make things right with her own mom.

"I don't think she knows that I know about you." Livy peeked up again. "What I told you about Dad letting it slip while he was drunk was the truth. Mom wasn't home when that happened."

Janie nodded. Inside, she seethed at the man who had recklessly twisted up their lives into a knotted mess. Had her father ever considered what his wandering irresponsibility had done to her? What it would do to Livy and Livy's mom?

Did he care?

She squished her rising resentment. "Hunter and I will figure this out. We'll get you back to your mom, okay?"

A pause lowered between them, and in it something undefined but meaningful loomed. Then Livy moved forward. She hugged Janie, timidly at first, but after a moment her arms tightened.

Janie wasn't sure what to do with that—how she felt. Was this kid playing her? She'd already proven to be dishonest. Was she manipulative too?

Even as the questions soured Janie's mind, a sense of something fierce settled into the uncertainty in her heart. It felt like . . . like loyalty.

Like love.

This was her sister. No matter who or what Livy proved to be, Janie's heart claimed her in that moment. For better or for worse.

CHAPTER FIFTEEN

BENNETT ZIPPED UP THE closure to his Nordic ski boot and pressed down the protective strap. It was crazy how different these were to the downhill boots. Lighter, sleeker. And the skis? Also different—long, skinny, and less rigid.

"It was convenient that MB had a few extra sets of these." Bennett glanced at Nathan, who was practicing stepping in and clicking out of the ski bindings. He focused intently on what he was doing, and the determination in his fixed jaw made Bennett smile.

"She used to rent them out to the few tourists who came to upper Elk Creek," Hazel said.

"Used to?"

Hazel shrugged. "We're pretty far off the beaten trail for tourism, and Nordic skiing isn't nearly as popular as downhill. Even so, Big Sky has both. I think the ski rentals ended up being more hassle than they were worth."

Bennett chuckled. "Not that you would complain about that."

An adorable, one-sided grin slipped onto that pretty mouth. "You know me so well."

Yeah, he did. But this? Something had come over Hazel. Something sweet and alluring—not that she hadn't already been attractive. Obviously Bennett found her very, very attractive. Enough to turn his life completely inside out for. But where he'd expected her to sulk and to punish him with withdrawn silence and well-aimed glares after he'd told her they needed to step back, she come at him with . . . gentleness. With a real try at friendship.

And when Hazel decided to try something, failure wasn't an option.

Electricity zipped through Bennett's veins as her hazel eyes collided with him and her half grin spread full. If he wasn't careful, he'd slip right back into flirting, and that would be a speedway back to full entanglement. At the moment he couldn't discern exactly why that would be a bad thing.

Not trusting his slipping thoughts, Bennett put his attention back on Nathan. "Think we can manage this?"

Nathan had both feet locked in the ski bindings. He planted both ski poles and lifted one slender stick off the ground. "Feet strapped to sticks, snow packed down like ice, and a gurgling, half-frozen river nearby. What could possibly go wrong?" His grin peeked through the coat he'd zipped up to his chin, and suddenly Nathan looked like a kid Bennett would want to hang out with, not a punk who pushed life toward the frustrating, difficult end of the spectrum.

Man, there must be some sort of magic up here in these hills.

Hazel stepped into her ski bindings and maneuvered beside Nathan, positioning herself between the boy and the river. "You'll not be going anywhere near the river, thank you very much."

Having a good two inches of height over Hazel, Nathan looked down at her. "I fully appreciate that you're going to be between me and hypothermia, but do you really think if things go awry, your ninety-something pounds are going to keep me from tumbling into freezing water?"

Hazel laughed. "Things won't go that awry, I promise." She pointed her camo glove toward the bend in the trail beyond. "There's a clearing just past there—that's our aim."

"Why didn't we go there before we strapped sticks to our feet?" Bennett asked.

"Because the slight incline will help you find a good feel for how to move. It's a good place to start."

Nathan and Bennett exchanged a glance, and Nathan shrugged. "You're the expert. Teach on, Teach."

"I'm moving up in the world."

"How's that?" Nathan asked.

"I used to go by badger lady." She cast a smirk toward Bennett. "*Teach* is an upgrade."

"You had to bring that up."

"Seriously?" Nathan raised his eyebrows as he looked at Bennett. "You called her *badger lady*?"

Bennett shrugged. "She sure did snarl at me when we first met."

"You were ridiculous when we first met."

"Did I mention she pushed me off a horse?"

"You fell off."

"Because you pushed me off."

"You learned real quick to use your legs to hold on."

Nathan laughed. "That's how she taught you to ride a horse?" He shook his head. "I might need to rethink this ski lesson thing . . ."

"No worries. You're not nearly as ridiculous—or as arrogant—as your brother was that day."

With a look first at Hazel and then pinned on Bennett, Nathan shook his head. "How did you two ever end up together?"

"We're not."

A half a beat after Hazel's response, silence stole the easy banter. Bennett shifted his look from Nathan's *I'm sorry* expression to Hazel's face.

She rolled her lips together, then tilted her head. "But we're friends. That's a long way in a good direction from where we started."

Even while pain oozed out of his cracked heart, a warm balm eased over the wound. "That's the truth."

A soft smile teased her lips, and she dipped the slightest nod. "So then, ready to ski?"

"I was born ready."

"I'll remind you of that Monday morning when it's time to get up for school." Bennett bumped Nathan's shoulder.

Nathan shrugged and pressed his weight forward, lifting a foot in an attempt to move. With the shift of his center of gravity, he wobbled, and before he could right the ship, he was on his side in the snow.

His laughter was a happy song in the forest. "Strike one."

"Wrong sport." Hazel reached for his hand and pulled him back to his feet, her own stance as steady as if she weren't strapped to the same sort of narrow sticks. "In this game, we generally don't swing sticks. Or strike out."

Bennett chuckled quietly. Soon enough he'd be in the snow too, so he wasn't about to poke fun.

Both feet solid beneath him, Nathan reset his poles. "Okay. How do we move forward."

"Let's start by you putting your poles in one hand and not using them."

"Why do I have them if I'm not going to use them?"

"You will. Just not yet."

"Okay." Nathan pulled the tips of his poles out of the snow and positioned them in one hand. "No poles. Now what?"

"Feet shoulder width apart."

"Wait. I know this one. Head down. Arms in. Knees apart." Nathan grinned.

"What? No. That's not how it works."

Bennett laughed. "She doesn't live on a steady stream of movies like your sister." He looked at Hazel. "He's quoting a Disney movie. *Tangled*."

"You should watch it. Bennett is a little bit like Flynn. Ridiculous. And can't ride a horse."

"Flynn can ride a horse!" Bennett said. "*I* can ride a horse."

"Focus, boys. We're skiing today."

"Right. But later we should watch *Tangled*."

Bennett stared at Nathan. "Who even are you right now?"

Nathan merely smiled. A bit of wonder, alongside a dump truck of gratitude, filled Bennett. *Can we keep this Nathan, God? It'd make life a whole lot easier . . .* He wondered if a *yes* would be more likely if this Ella Harmond girl was in the picture. Meeting her bumped up on the priority list.

Hazel regained command and gave both Nathan and Bennett some basic instructions on stance. Then they were shuffling—slowly—getting a feel for balance. Once they'd shuffled their way up to the bend where a wide meadow was covered with snow—a journey that took about eight times longer than it seemed it should have—Hazel had both boys employ their ski poles and work on incorporating a glide into their shuffling.

Round and round they went. Shuffling. Trying to glide. Learning how to move with long sticks strapped to their feet. By the time it seemed they'd gotten a feel for Nordic skiing, both Nathan and Bennett had shed their heavy coats, and Bennett's breaths came and went in fast, heavy puffs.

"I think that's enough for today," Hazel announced. "Likely you'll be sore tonight."

"Tonight?" Bennett leaned back, attempting to work the tight knots in his back and hamstrings loose. "That train has left the station, lady."

"You're just old, Bennett." Nathan shuffled onward into another lap. "I could do this all day."

"That's good, because that's sort of what you've sign up for." Hazel snatched Nathan's coat from a pine branch. "But I'm hungry, and it's soup night at Janie's Café."

Bennett grabbed his coat and pushed his arms into the sleeves but left it unzipped. "Taco soup, according to Hunter. I'm not missing that."

Halfway through his lap, Nathan waved. "Go ahead. I'll catch up."

With a glance at Hazel, Bennett caught her nod.

"He's doing well—he'll be fine," she said.

"Good enough for me." Bennett motioned for her to lead the way. Over his shoulder, and using a teasing tone, he called back to Nathan. "Stick to the trail, eh, bud? Remember the last time you wandered off . . ."

Hazel whapped him in the gut with the back of her hand. "Don't ruin a good day."

Bennett couldn't help but wink. Man, flirting with her came as easy as breathing . . . as did the longing for things that went well past *friends*.

Hazel skied in front of him with practiced ease. He enjoyed watching the smooth movements of her lithe body. What had her brother been thinking all those years, letting her work as a solo hunting guide for a clientele of mostly men? Hazel was as attractive in snow gear in the middle of a mountain forest as any woman he'd ever seen in sleek silk at a posh resort.

Yeah, friendship wasn't at the forefront of his mind at all. He knew what it was like to hold that little mountain fox in his arms. He knew the thrill of her breath mingled with his, the intoxication of her kisses, the way her touch electrified his body. The simple memory of it knocked his pulse back up to what it had been while pushing through awkward laps back at the meadow. When she reached the parking lot at the trailhead, his breaths came in quick puffs of white all over again.

"It's a decent workout, isn't it?"

Thrashing in this physical attraction to his ski teacher, trying to keep *friends* firmly in the place of *lovers*? Yes. It was proving to be one of the most taxing workouts of his life.

***

Hazel had her feet unbound from her skis and was loading them on top of Bennett's Jeep. The day had gone perfectly. Brilliant sunshine in the deep-blue sky. Snow glittering against the trees. The trail had been nicely packed for a new Nordic skier. And the first go at it with Nathan and Bennett had been flawless.

Even so, the strange stirring in her heart hadn't let up. It wasn't uncomfortable, per se, but it was . . . odd.

Had the starry night been singing? Whatever had happened, the unfamiliar wonder of it hadn't released its grip.

Bennett brushed beside her, lifting his skis into the flat carrier. She glanced up at him, finding his jaw tight. Had he not enjoyed the afternoon?

His skis settled, he looked down and caught her staring. He pushed his hands into his pockets, but his eyes didn't waver from hers. The intensity of those beautiful blue eyes made her heart skip, and Hazel stepped back, lowering her gaze.

"Thank you for today, Zel."

Was there a reason his voice sounded so rough? Hazel pushed passed the uncertainty and reached for the friendship she'd promised this man. Summoning a smile, she looked back up at him. "I had fun. I hope you and Nathan did too—you both did really well."

For an achingly beautiful moment, his expression softened, becoming the sort she'd been familiar with in their tender and intimate moments. Yearning stretched in her chest. She moved her focus to the trail and the river, behind Bennett. "Think Nathan is taking another lap before he meets us?"

Bennett looked toward the river. "Maybe. He seems to really like this." He shook his head. "Who knew he watched Disney movies?"

Hazel leaned against the car. "Or could banter without a sharp edge."

He turned back to her. "You seem to bring out the best in him."

"Aren't we all full of surprises."

Though his expression still seemed guarded, Bennett smiled. For a stretch of several heartbeats, their conversation melted into the quiet movement of the trees and river. A swish of a gentle breeze through the pines. The gurgle of water flowing beneath a blanket of ice. The chattering of a bird somewhere high up in the treetops. And Bennett's steady, tender gaze.

Beauty all around. Peace spread like an invitation.

"Can I ask you something?" Hazel said.

Bennett blinked, as if she'd pulled him out of a soft trance. "Of course."

"Have you ever . . ." She sighed, wondering if he'd think she was crazy. Or just enormously lonely. Maybe both.

"Have I ever . . ." He waited for her to finish her open-ended query.

"The other night I went out to the dock to look at the stars."

"Sounds normal for you. You have quite the view for star gazing." Bennett lifted a lopsided grin. "A habit I've picked up."

For some reason, that made her happy. How far he'd come, this city boy who had been afraid of the dark.

"Was there something new?" he pressed.

Hazel ducked, tucking her hands into her pockets as she studied their boot prints in the snow. "Yes. It was . . . strange. And amazing."

"What?"

"The sky. It . . . was like it sang." Heat flooded her cheeks, and she hoped he could only see the stocking cap on the top of her head.

"It sang? Like how?"

He didn't sound mocking. Or disbelieving. Hazel lifted her eyes to find him watching her.

"Not like a choir or something. Not even really something that I could hear with my ears. But I heard it"—she tapped her chest—"here."

His grin grew wide, and those blue eyes lit. "You didn't hear audible voices? But *felt* the stars sing?"

What she *felt* at the moment was ridiculous. "Don't laugh at me."

One hand came free of his coat pocket, and he covered her shoulder with it. "I'm not laughing, Zel. Honest. That's amazing."

"Amazing?" She shook her head. "I think it's insane."

"The Bible talks about the stars singing praises to God. I recently read it in Job."

Hazel blinked. Stars singing? What was this madness? "That . . . that's not something I believe."

"But you heard singing."

"Maybe I was remembering something from my childhood, and I was tired. Emotional." She glanced at him and stepped away. "I've been kind of a wreck, to be honest."

Bennett's lips tucked together tightly, and he flinched.

"That's not meant to make you feel bad."

He nodded. "I know."

"Actually, I think you were probably right about us."

"About this?" He motioned between them.

She understood he meant this stumbling friendship and nodded. "Yes. It's . . . it's surprisingly more comfortable than I thought. Easier."

Bennett visibly swallowed, and his slight nod was delayed. He didn't feel the same? Was that why he'd been withdrawn earlier? Was he detaching himself from her even more?

The possibility triggered a painful panic. But what could she do about it?

"You keep surprising me," Bennett whispered.

Jarred yet again, Hazel stared at him. Finally a wisp of a smile resurfaced on his strained mouth. "Thank you for making such a good effort. And for everything you're doing with Nathan. I can't tell you how much it means to me." His eyes held sincerity and warmth.

Once again her heart reached toward him with a painful yearning. Yes, friendship had been easier than she'd thought. But that didn't diminish how much she loved this man and wanted more with him. So much more.

"Tell me more about this song." He leaned back against the Jeep, crossing his arms over his chest. "If it was a memory, do you know where it was from?"

Back to reaching for comfortable friendship again, then. Although this topic wasn't exactly like talking about the weather or anything else normal and mundane. Even so, if she couldn't tell Bennett, who could she tell? And if she couldn't tell Bennett, did they really have a hope for more again someday?

Hazel shut her eyes and reached back for the anthem of that night. "There were words—but that part I know was a memory." She looked at him. "It wasn't the same."

"What was the memory?"

"My nan singing. She did sometimes—more when I was little than when I was older."

"Do you remember the words?"

Feeling vulnerable and silly, Hazel swallowed. Nodded. And then took a deep breath. "*Lord, how your wonders are displayed, where'er we turn our eyes, if we survey the ground we tread or gaze upon the skies.*"

Astonishment lifted Bennett's brow. "That sounds like a hymn."

"Nan would listen to records sometimes. I think it was on one."

"I'll bet my mom would know which hymn, if we asked her."

Hazel shook her head. "No. I don't want to do that."

"Why not?"

"Bennett, this is silly enough as it is. Who knows what your mom thinks of me already."

"I don't think it's silly."

"You don't think I'm losing my mind?"

He shook his head, unfolding his arms, and took a step nearer. "No. I don't think you're losing anything. Maybe you're *finding* something. Something that matters for eternity."

Hazel looked toward her boots and nearly cowered beneath his intensity. After several moments, she blinked back tears she had zero explanation for and shook her head. "It was just a beautiful night."

Bennett's stare fell, and he stepped back. "Beauty has a purpose, Hazel."

She shook her head again. It was too out there. Too big and beyond her to think about.

CHAPTER SIXTEEN

As HE WAITED IN the window booth at Janie's Café for the guys, Bennett hit Replay on the YouTube video, the music strong and captivating in his ears.

"I Sing the Mighty Power of God." That had been what Hazel had been quoting—the hymn from her memory. He'd typed in the lyrics she'd recited and let Google do its magic. She'd had the second verse near to perfect.

That was quite a memory. And the Ball Brothers sang Isaac Watts's rich song with stirring emotion. Perhaps that was aided by the wonder of it all—that Hazel's soul had heard the music of the stars, that her nan had sung hymns of praise in her childhood, and that she remembered it.

That was quite a development. Miraculous, really.

Bennett tried to temper his wildly racing hope—that for Hazel's awakening soul. But what else could it be? Was there any other explanation but that God was breathing life into her soul?

Please, God . . .

Even as he sent that silent plea heavenward, he wondered how often his mother had done the very same—her entreaties lifted for his own stony heart.

Praise God for a faithful, relentless mother.

Praise God for His faithful, relentless love.

Bennett closed his eyes and let the music blend with the gratitude of his soul and offered both up as worship.

"While all that borrows life from you

is ever in your care,

and everywhere that we can be,

you, God, are present there."

The final verse blended on the talented voices of three men as the tinkling of the bell jingled into the music. Bennett removed his earbuds and closed the YouTube app, then stood. José walked toward him, followed by Hunter. When Bennett stuck out his hand, José swatted it away and moved to wrap him in a bear hug instead.

"It's been a while, my friend. Too long."

Bennett returned the strong embrace and patted José's back. "I agree. These winter mountain roads are a bit of an inconvenience."

José stepped back and shrugged, a hint of discouragement in the action. "Life."

Hunter stepped around them both and slid into the booth opposite of where Bennett had been. José sat next to Hunter, and Bennett regained his seat. "John said he'd have to miss this one, but he sent a prayer. I'll read it when we finish our study."

Hunter nodded. "Pastor Nolan said he'd make it."

"*Excelente!*" José clapped his hands together and rubbed them with eagerness, though something reserved seemed to temper his enthusiasm. "I've been missing this."

"Bennett says you have a fairly large church in Bozeman."

"We do, and it's good. But there's nothing like brothers. The kind that you trust with *tu alma*." He tapped his chest with his fist. "With your soul."

Wonder deepened as Bennett silently agreed. *Brotherhood.* Never had that in his life. Not once. His existence before his head-injury wake-up call seemed so shallow and empty when he looked back on it from this side. How ironic was that? He'd been a man of envy—money, success, women—and had it all. And yet he'd had nothing. Nothing compared to the riches he knew now.

Emotion gripped hard, and he had to work a steady breath before he could speak.

"While we wait," he said, relieved his voice didn't wobble, "I have a question for you guys."

"Shoot."

"Do you think our souls can hear nature sing?"

Hunter's brows shot up. "Interesting."

José tipped his head to one side, pondering. "Nature sing . . ."

"Like the Christmas song—let heaven and nature sing?" Hunter asked.

"Like in the book of Job, where it says that the morning stars sang together."

"Think that is talking about literal stars?" José asked.

Bennett shrugged, feeling exposed. No wonder Hazel had been certain he'd been laughing at her—which he hadn't been. At all. He'd been gobsmacked, in a good way. "I don't know. I'm asking you guys."

Still wearing deep thought, José nodded. "It's a good question. The psalms tell us that the heavens declare the glory of God and the firmament proclaims His handiwork. *Los cielos cuentan la gloria de Dios, el firmamento proclama la obra de sus manos.* My mama still quotes that verse every morning as the sun comes up." He folded his hands and stretched them on the table. "Want to tell us where this is coming from?"

Bennett considered his words carefully. "Just a conversation I had with Hazel the other day. It was something personal, so I can't tell you about it, really. But it made me think . . . Does God speak to our souls through nature?"

Hunter nodded, as if he suddenly understood. He would. Next to Bennett, he knew Hazel better than anyone. "Mama B once told me that God whispers to us in a language that is personal—one we can hear and understand."

"What was the context of that?"

"I think she was reading. She said she understood life through story, and God spoke to her using story."

Bennett thought on that. It made sense—hadn't Jesus taught through story? But then, what about through nature? Did God speak through nature? Had He *sung* through the night sky for Hazel? Or maybe she'd been given a glimpse—or whatever it would be for hearing rather than seeing—into the praise of the cosmos? Something that her wild, nature-loving heart would hear and understand?

With everything he had, he hoped that one way or another, God was awakening her soul. But he didn't want to misrepresent God to Hazel's wandering soul.

"Just to clarify, we're not talking about pantheism here, right?" José asked.

"I don't even know what that means," Hunter said.

"God manifested as the universe—as nature." Bennett shook his head. "No, that's not what I'm talking about. I mean God revealing Himself *through* nature, not God being in all and all being God."

"Sounds like we're already into it." Pastor Nolan squeezed Bennett's shoulders from behind.

How had Bennett not heard the sound of Janie's bell above the door? Pastor was right—they were deep in it. He moved over toward the window, making space for the man to sit next to him.

Nolan slid into the spot Bennett had vacated. "What have I missed?"

Hunter connected with Bennett's glance, a question in that quick look. Bennett appreciated that Hunter wanted to protect his little sister, and Bennett dipped a small nod, wordlessly agreeing that they should.

Hunter gestured toward Bennett. "Bennett asked a question about nature speaking to us about God. If that was a thing."

A good way of putting it without dragging Hazel into it. Bennett wasn't sure that Nolan shouldn't know about Hazel's experience the other night—of the four men sitting there, he was the theologian. He would know better what to say about it. But Bennett was certain that Hazel wouldn't be fond of him betraying her trust—after all, she was so worried that Bennett had been laughing at her, and she was much more familiar with him than the pastor.

Truth be known, Bennett felt a little small and silly himself, sitting there asking such questions. Pastor seemed like a giant to him. A man of infallible faith next to a boy who'd gotten himself so lost that he'd become afraid of the dark and deaf to the God who had offered the way back. The comparison knotted cords of discomfort in Bennett's gut.

"Nature is our evidence of God and proof of His power." Nolan looked at Bennett, no trace of laughter or disapproval in his kind eyes. "So yes. I'd say that's a thing. A very biblical thing."

Bennett nodded, not sure that they were talking about the same thing, exactly. "What about something more . . . explicit than a general revelation of order and design. Something more . . . supernatural. More intimate."

"I think you're going to have to be a little more specific with that one," Nolan said.

"Can the stars sing—the cosmos have music—that one could hear? I mean, not physically hear with our ears, but . . . but sense." Bennett tapped his chest. "Feel in here."

Pastor rubbed his chin, his expression intrigued. "Interesting."

Hunter nodded. "That's what I said."

"What do you think, Hunt? After all, you grew up in the middle of this wild wonder. Spent most of your life traipsing mountain trails. Is this something you've ever experienced?"

Hunter looked at his hands, pressed on the table, and thought quietly for several moments. Then he shook his head. "Not the way that my—that Bennett is talking about."

"How did you come to know God? To believe in Christ?"

"John Brighton."

"He told you?"

Hunter nodded.

"With just words?"

Again, Hunter hesitated. "No. Not just with words. I saw something in his life. A peace and a faithfulness. Joy. Steadfastness. And for some reason, he invested in me. Came to visit me on Sunday evenings. Started inviting me over for dinners or desserts, even though he outranked me by far."

Nolan nodded. "So would you say God spoke to you through John Brighton?"

"Yeah, I think that would be accurate."

"But when you came to believe, to accept Christ as your Savior, was it only because of what you saw in John?"

"No. He told me how to be saved. He showed me in the Bible what it says about how I could have a relationship with God. *Believe on the Lord Jesus Christ*—that's in Acts, right?"

Again, Nolan nodded, a small, proud smile tipping his lips. "So then, God reached your heart through both—through creation, that being a man, and through His Word. I think Paul would confirm this dual action in Romans."

With that, they were off. Digging into their Bibles. Bennett followed carefully, but the question still niggled in the back of his mind: *Did You sing to her? Or maybe allow her to hear the music of the stars? Are You calling her?*

He'd never wanted more for the royal answer to be *yes*.

An hour later, the men closed their Bibles as Janie refilled their coffee mugs. She did so with a smile, though she didn't say much.

Didn't want to interrupt. Bennett didn't miss the wink Hunter sent her way or the pleased blush that colored her cheeks.

A thin thread of envy pulled through him. They were so happy now. And so unashamedly in love. Bennett craved such a tender, trusting relationship with Hazel.

Friends was going okay though. More than okay. Hazel had embraced it, making the transition so much easier—better—than Bennett had expected. Maybe someday . . .

Bennett gently folded that thought and tucked it away. *Friends* was what he'd asked for from Hazel and all they could have right now. Though he couldn't list out all the reasons, he knew firmly in his heart that was the simple truth.

"Before Hunter reads John's closing prayer for us, how can we pray for each other in the coming weeks?" Pastor asked.

José sat straight even as he shifted in his seat. He met Bennett's look with a dark, sad warning. "Pray for my sister, will you?"

"Is Isa okay?"

With his jaw tightening, José lowered his head and then shook it. "I don't know for sure. She's . . . she's gone rogue. She started seeing some guy we know nothing about." He looked up, fear creasing his brow. "I haven't talked to her in a week. She's not answering texts or calls."

Ice lodged in Bennett's chest. Why would Isa do that?

"My parents are terrified and hurt. I'm angry and hurt. I've done some digging into the man she's gotten involved with, and I haven't liked what I've found."

"Is he dangerous?" Hunter asked, his fierce warrior-protector side emerging instantly. Bennett saw why Hunter had gone into the military—it would have suited Hunter's natural bend to guard what he valued, to defend what should be kept safe.

José's jaw clenched again. "I'm not certain on that. But he's married. She cut off contact when I confronted her with that."

Bennett's heart dropped like a stone. *Dear God, what has Isa gotten herself into?*

"Thing is, Isa is an adult. By age at least." José rubbed his head. "There is nothing we can do."

Hunter gripped the man's shoulder, and Nolan reached across the table to grasp his elbow. "We can pray."

Bennett nodded, and they did exactly that right then and there. Even so, hopeless sorrow weighed in his spirit. He couldn't imagine how José ached at this. Or the elder Romeros. They loved Isa fiercely.

And Isa mattered to Bennett as well. She'd become a friend. Like a sister. If this was Gemma they were talking about . . .

His head nearly exploded at that thought. Righteous anger might become *un*righteous real fast if Bennett ever encountered a scoundrel who would do such a thing to his little sister.

A man like his own father. In truth, a man not too much *un*like the one Bennett had been not so very long ago.

Burning nausea twisted his gut. Why were people so easily led into destruction? He didn't have an answer. Just the deep, heart-piercing knowledge that they were. Every one of them.

He knew this intimately. He'd done a bang-up job of it himself.

CHAPTER
SEVENTEEN

"THINGS BETWEEN YOU AND my sister seem . . . quiet." Hunter hefted a box filled with various hardware, an odd tool or two, and more masking tape than would likely be used in Luna in a year's time. Why had Stamps Hardware had so much in stock?

From what he could remember—which wasn't much—Mr. Stamps had been an odd duck. An eclectic, disorganized odd duck—confirmed by the variety in excess they'd found while cleaning and sorting the long-since-closed store.

He and Bennett were nearly finished moving the boxes of dust-covered goods that had been left on shelves and in bins into the attic. Tara Crofton had framers lined up for the week after Christmas, all set to come and transform the old hardware store into her clinic. Hunter had told her he'd help whenever he could, even volunteering to do the framing for free. She'd waved off that offer, saying she'd hire a contractor.

Hunter wasn't sure if that was distrust in his ability to square two-by-fours or if she hadn't wanted to take advantage of her son's friend. Either way, she'd hired out. But had accepted help moving the old goods, once she'd sorted it and packed it away.

Bennett grunted as he lifted a box full of *Do It Better Yourself* manuals and old *Handyman* magazines. "Yeah. Quiet in a good way, I think."

"Meaning no more explosive fights?" Hunter chuckled. When it came to Hazel, he was acquainted with the gunpowder behind her temper.

Bennett shrugged. "I don't know that we had explosive fights. Just issues we couldn't resolve." Pain flickered in the glance he cast toward Hunter, and Hunter felt bad for teasing him. "But no, I don't even really mean that. Relationships are going to have tension. People fight, you know? We are all selfish sometimes. It's just life. You know that wasn't the reason I suggested we step back."

"It wasn't?"

"No. I can deal with disagreements."

Conversation stalled while both men clomped up the narrow stairway, their muscles straining against the burdens they hefted. Once in the attic, Bennett resumed the topic. "I've been at the negotiating table enough to know that most, if not all, disagreements can be resolved if both parties have the same goal."

"And you and Hazel didn't have the same goal?" Hunter followed him toward the north wall, near one of the two dormered windows on that side. "I mean, you both clearly miss each other. You want to be together. You don't count that?"

"No." Bennett lowered the straining box onto the freshly swept sheeting of the attic floor. "I want marriage. Hazel doesn't. I'm willing to wait, but when she suggested we move in together . . ." He shook his head as color stained his cheeks above his thick beard. "That was a gut punch—to realize the best she thought of me was live-in boyfriend. No promises, you know? I can't live like that. Maybe the guy I was before could, but now . . ." He shook his head.

Hunter got that. Bennett had had a drastic change-course collision with God. One that, whether Hazel admitted it or not, made him the man she loved. It also made him one she couldn't comprehend.

"Right now that's not reconcilable. And beyond that, my faith and her rejection of God aren't compatible. Where does that leave us?"

That was it exactly. A big part of Hunter wanted to brush that aside—claim that Hazel would get there eventually, and it would all be okay. Love conquers all. But it wasn't that easy. His faith made Bennett as attractive to Hazel as incomprehensible.

Would she ever get that?

Bennett lifted his baseball cap, exposing his long dark hair to the chill of the room, shook out the curls, and replaced the hat. He rolled his shoulders and then squared to Hunter as he lowered his box onto the one Bennett had just set down. "Don't misunderstand me, Hunter. I love her. Hazel's it for me, and I'm always going to love her. I'm not moving on. But she and I are not going the same direction right now. That can't lead anywhere good."

The familiar tug of deep pity pulled in Hunter's chest—for both Hazel and Bennett. Because he could see how much this wrecked Bennett—and Hunter understood that pain. Seven years of loving a woman who hadn't been going the same direction he had been was well enough proof of what Bennett was saying.

Even so, Hunter couldn't help but cling to the scraps of hope he had for Hazel and Bennett. Maybe it *was* working out. Just a long, hard process . . . "Tell me about what happened with Hazel and the stars."

Bennett shook his head. "I can't do that to her. She told me in confidence—maybe I shouldn't have even brought it up the other day at study. But I don't know enough of the Bible to know for sure if I'm thinking right, and it's too important to be misleading Hazel, even if it's unintentional."

"Okay, fair enough." Hunter rocked back on his heels, hope rising like heat from a fire. "But I guess what I'm shooting at is that it's an encouraging sign, don't you think? I mean, Hazel's never once wondered about God before this year. Whenever MB or Nana would bring Him up, she would get this stony look and walk away."

Thumbs hooked on his pockets, Bennett leaned against the wide plank of the window frame. "I'm working really hard not to get ahead of myself with that. The truth is, I'm the one who brought up God when she told me about the stars."

Hunter nodded, hope undeterred. "But she didn't wall up."

"Well, she said that she didn't believe that sort of stuff . . . but she wasn't very convincing. And she said she remembered something your nan used to sing. She didn't know what it was, but she was able to recite a full verse. A hymn."

"She remembered the words?"

"Yeah."

That was incredible. All these years Hazel had denied God outright, resented when anything about God had been brought up, and claimed that if there was a God, He wasn't fair, didn't care about people, and wasn't worth her thinking about.

But she remembered one of Nan's hymns. And she was reading Nan's books.

"I'm going to take all of that as a good sign." Hunter clapped a hand onto Bennett's shoulder. "I get why you're cautious. But I have to tell you something—I found her several weeks back, up at the Black Gulch. She was reading a C. S. Lewis book—one that was really challenging her."

Bennett stared at him, hope shaping his expression.

Hunter held up a hand. "I'm not trying to shovel in false hope, but I'm thinking God got to you. He got to me. A pair of hard-headed, stiff-necked men bent on doing our own thing. Put us in our place—right on our knees so He could show us His grace. It's not too much to think He can get to Hazel too. Even if it means a night symphony for one to do it."

Now back to a leaned-in posture in the window, with his head bent, Bennett nodded. "I know."

"You sound less than thrilled."

"No, I am thrilled. But it feels . . . heavy." He brought his face up. "I don't want to screw up anymore. I messed up things between her and me already. Gave her the impression that live-in boyfriend was the best I could be. But this is bigger than my happiness. Bigger than the fact that I wish she wanted to marry me. This is eternity we're talking about. Hazel's eternity. And she's asking me questions. Me. The guy who walked away from God in anger. The guy it took losing his memory before he had the sense to come back. What if I mess up again?"

Hunter's enthusiasm sobered as Bennett shared the weight he shouldered. Made Hunter think of something he'd recently read in a C. S. Lewis book *The Weight of Glory*, in which Lewis wrote about the daily weight of his neighbor's soul—one so precious and heavy that only humility would bear it. Because people weren't *ordinary*. Not mere mortals.

Eternity mattered for every soul.

Bennett was carrying that weight—and it was clearly heavy—well. Hazel's *soul* was precious to him—even more so than their relationship. That took an eternal view—and a whole lot of humility.

"Seems God is trusting you with this, Bennett."

Bennett winced.

Hunter nodded, more convinced of what he'd just said than when he'd said it. "Hazel trusts you too. You'll tell her the truth, even when she doesn't want to hear it."

"I want her to hear it though."

"Apparently so does God."

Bennett swallowed hard, staring at Hunter with a mix of fear and hope.

"I think John would tell you to keep your eyes on Jesus. Follow Him, and you won't go wrong."

A slow, solemn nod. "You'll pray for me, right?"

"You know it." Hunter lowered onto the top of the box he'd set down. "And speaking of praying, I've been thinking about Isa." An awkward transition to an awkward subject.

"Yeah, me too. Her family has got to be heartbroken." Bennett shook his head and rolled a fist. "She knows better. She really does. I warned her last summer that she needed to be careful."

Hunter nodded, not sure what to say to Bennett's intensity. If Hazel were there right then, she might have misread Bennett's reaction. Hunter tried hard not to do the same. Even while he cautioned himself, a sense of obligation pressed—one that had been doing so since the day José had told them.

"I keep feeling like I'm supposed to help somehow," Hunter said.

Bennett stood up from the windowpane. "That sounds . . . like potential trouble." A look of warning followed.

Hunter's face warmed. He knew exactly what Bennett was thinking. "It wasn't her fault, exactly."

"She hung on your arm, flirted openly, and it made Janie crazy." One eyebrow arched. "You told me you hadn't meant to—"

"I didn't. I promise I wasn't trying to make Janie jealous. It was just a situation that spiraled out of control. But I don't think that Isa meant to make things go the way they did. I mean, what did she really know about me and Janie and all our history? From her view, Janie was with Grady, and I was fair game. She wasn't trying to cause trouble."

"No. I doubt she was. Isa is just . . ." Bennett blew out a breath. "I don't know what she is. A flirt for sure. But not the sultry kind. Not the kind that goes around trying to wreck others. I think she just wants to be loved."

"Don't we all."

Bennett walked toward the stairs, no doubt intending to get another box. They had a lot of work left to do.

"Bennett?"

"Yeah."

"You think I'm wrong? To feel like I'm supposed to help Isa somehow?"

"No." Now halfway down the stairs, Bennett turned and looked up at him. His hesitation was strained, but then he shook his head. "No I don't. To tell the truth, I've been pressed with the same thing. It's just . . . I don't see that going well. With Janie or with Hazel."

Hunter blew out a long sigh. "No kidding. I haven't brought it up with Janie yet." He rubbed his neck, feeling every bit the coward.

"Better do that first. Might be a moot point though. By the sounds of it, Isa doesn't want help."

"I was wondering how long it would take you to find your way across that road." Mama held a raised-brow look on Janie. Borderline *squinty eyes*.

A fresh twist of guilt knotted Janie's stomach. She shouldn't have let more than a week pass since painting the lodge before she came to talk to Mama. In her defense, she was a busy business owner with a live-in guest and was in the throes of planning her wedding on top of that. She wasn't avoiding Mama. Exactly.

"I brought you a hot cocoa bomb." Janie held out her peace offering and smiled. Maybe that was a touch manipulative.

Mama's eyes grinned, even if she kept her lips pinned down neatly as she shook her head. "That's my girl." She waved her toward the stairway. "Come up and we'll talk."

Janie followed Mama up the familiar stairway to the apartment above the Pantry. They passed the open room to the right, where the punching bag still hung, and for the first time in her life, Janie wondered if Mama had hung it there for herself and not just for a trio of teenage kids who'd had some things they needed to work through.

At the end of the short hall, Mama opened the door, and they passed into Janie's childhood home. It had never occurred to her that it might be strange to live above her mama's store. She didn't even know what a *commute* was until she was an adult. In so many ways, she'd been sheltered from life outside Luna.

Perhaps that was why she couldn't get over her dad's departure. Her friends—most of them—had both parents around. Even if often one of those parents traveled elsewhere to make a living—a whole different sort of commute than what she discovered was commonly meant—her friends had *contact* with both mom and dad. She'd felt so . . . so left out when other girls talked about their *daddies*. So jilted when the other kids complained about how unfair their parents were.

It was one of the bonding points she had with the Wallace siblings. They got it. Except their parents hadn't vanished willingly. Not like her father.

"Let's just clear the air so we can enjoy the mountain crispness God put us in." Mama set her hot cocoa bomb on the small round table in the eat-in kitchen. "I don't like lies, Janie girl. You know that."

"We talked about this already."

"I know it. And I forgive you. But I want it to be clear as Elk Lake in July. I *do not* like lies. It's not how you and I have lived, and I don't want to start something different now."

"Okay. I hear you." Janie glanced toward the small rocker set near the south-facing window, where it would be bathed in the late-afternoon sunshine. At this hour, that warm drenching of light had past. But there was still enough daylight for her to glimpse a book lying open on the floor near the wall.

She hadn't seen that in years. Not since she was a girl.

Her heart squeezed as she looked back to Mama. "That's the old photo album."

"Yes, it is." Mama held her gaze.

"I haven't seen that since . . ." Since about a year after Dad had left.

"I know."

Janie crossed her arms. "I knew it would bother you, Mama. That was why—"

"Sometimes a person has to work through old memories all over again." Mama stepped forward.

"I was trying to save you from that."

Mama's eyes softened as she reached across the small distance left between them, laying her hand on Janie's forearm. "I know that. But I would rather you be honest with me. And I'll be honest with you. It was hard at first, turning those pages, seeing those images from back then. I'd almost forgotten what he looked like. Seeing him smiling, you cuddled in his lap, made me cry. But Janie girl? Sometimes we have to cry. Sometimes we have to let ourselves grieve—even if we thought we were past it all."

"Mama," Janie whispered. "I don't want to make you cry. I remember how much you did after he left. I know you thought I didn't see it, but I did."

Mama tugged her into a hug. "They were hard days, weren't they?"

With a tear rolling down her nose, Janie nodded.

"But we got through them." Mama patted her shoulder and stepped back. "And we'll get through this."

With her fingertips, Janie swiped away the wetness on her cheek. "I sure hope so." She drew in a long breath and let it out with a shaking exhale. "That is one of the things I wanted to come tell you. Livy needs to go back. Turns out she wasn't honest about her mom—which is a long story that I'm not going into right now—and she needs to get home. Hunter and I don't like the idea of her driving all that way by herself, so we've decided to go with her, and then we'll fly back next week. Bennett says he'll pick us up in Billings."

Mama took all that in without flinching. "I think that's the best thing to do. Do you have someone to cover the café, or will you close it for the week?"

"Tara says she'll cover again—at least the mornings. Gemma volunteered to help, in her usually bright-as-the-sun enthusiasm."

Mama chuckled at that. "Then it's worked out."

Janie nodded. For a moment she looked down at the old shag carpet and allowed years to blend into that moment. She'd raced around this floor with her mom, playing monster or tag or just running to get the wiggles out. She'd lain on her belly with a puzzle on a posterboard in front of her, spending hours matching colorful pieces until they formed a picture.

Long ago she'd tumbled on the floor with her dad. The memory was faint but still recognizable. He'd taught her how to do a summersault one night, after they'd watched the gymnastics competition in the summer Olympics. In that memory, she could hear his deep laughter.

She shivered against the resulting pain.

"Janie."

Clenching her fists, she looked at her mom with a forced smile.

"There were good times."

How did Mama always seem to read her mind?

"Yeah. A few."

"If you see your dad, remember that. We had some good days. Good memories."

Janie blinked, her attention wandering back to that old photo album. "Is that what you were looking for?"

Mama shrugged. "Like I said, I was just processing. And it was good for me. Because I saw them captured in print. Those good times. We had them." She stepped close and wrapped a strong arm around Janie's shoulders. "And I have you. That's a gift, and I'm always going to be grateful."

CHAPTER EIGHTEEN

HAZEL STROKED SCOUT'S HEAD, mindlessly running her fingers through the warmth of the dog's soft fur as she listened to the vocal blending of voices from the spinning vinyl on her grandparents' record player.

She hadn't cracked open the old wooden case in years. Hadn't dug out the sleeves containing the black vinyl disks. Even when she had—that first year she was entirely alone after Nan had died and Hunter had left—this record hadn't been one she'd played.

Not the Gaithers and their gospel music.

But she couldn't budge those lyrics from her mind. Bennett had texted her the night she'd told him about the . . . music. Said he'd googled the lyrics and they were from a hymn called "I Sing the Mighty Power of God." Sent her a link to a YouTube version by some good-looking brothers. She'd listened to it a few times and enjoyed the blending of their voices.

Made her think of the vinyl. Was that song on one Nan had played?

So far, no. But as she listened to the soft popping of that spinning disk underscore the rich music of other songs, memories of Nan resurfaced as though they were only moments past, not years.

Jesus sees what is lost and saves those who are willing.

That one. Nan had whispered those words to Hazel the night when Mom and Dad hadn't come back from their climb. Little Girl Hazel had clung to that promise. And when it had proved false . . .

Little Girl Hazel's heart had hardened to granite. As tough and cold as the Black Gulch that had claimed her parents' lives. And that had been fine by her.

But stone could crack. And something in her was cracking.

Hazel had fought against it. Denied it. Railed at it. But there it was. The truth. The hard casing crusted around her heart had fractured, exposing the fleshy pain hidden within.

Because of Bennett?

She couldn't say for sure. And that wasn't the real issue. She was frightened to discover what was inside. Worse, terrified to let anything touch the tender, untried center.

Even Bennett.

A horrible scratch ripped the air as the needle slid across the vinyl. Scrambling up from the kitchen chair, she crossed the small cabin and flung the needle away before it did more damage. Silence filled the space that had rang with music.

Scout crossed the room, her nails a pit-pat on the wood floor, and then sat to smile up at Hazel. Her happy eyes, always ready for adventure, beckoned Hazel to leave the confusion of her thoughts, the tomb of silence that had become her cabin.

"You're right." Hazel nodded at Scout. "It's a beautiful day out, and we aren't doing anything useful in here."

Tail bouncing, Scout stood, a signal to Ice and Cream. All three dogs bounded for the front door. Hazel met them there while putting on her winter coat. She turned to the old quilt spread on the floor for the dogs and found Moose unmoved by the younger three's enthusiasm to leave.

"You coming, old man?"

Moose lifted his head but didn't do more to get up. *Nope. I'm good here.*

"Nathan's coming out after school," she coaxed. Moose was spending more and more time in the cabin. An alarming trend.

His big, furry ears twitched. *That's nice.* That was it.

"Bennett too."

That big head popped up again. This time his eyes sparked. *Yeah?*

"Is that what it takes?" Hazel frowned. "Are you sulking? Because he hasn't been around as much?"

Moose looked away. *I don't know what you're talking about.*

"Good grief." She shook her head. At the dog and at herself. Was it really that shocking that she thought she heard the stars sing? She had two-way conversations with her dogs all the time.

Maybe she was crazy.

Maybe you're finding something. Bennett's response seeped into her heart. The one that was breaking open. The fissure grew a little more, and something warm pulsed inside.

Not willing to examine that, Hazel opened the front door, waited for the three younger dogs to clamber their way into the snow, and addressed Moose again. "I'll let you know when he gets here. Does that suit you?"

Moose's tongue slid out of his mouth as he panted happily. Hazel couldn't help but chuckle.

With the three dogs running haphazardly around the outside of the cabin, stopping to wrestle or roll in the snow every few minutes, Hazel walked to the tack room.

"Hi there, Mr. Big." The large paint nickered back as she opened the gate. "You and Pony staying warm enough?"

A puff of white snorted from the little horse's nostrils. What that meant, Hazel wasn't sure. She didn't speak equine as fluently as canine. More's the pity.

Hazel moved the tack room door, grinning at that handy new latch that would let her in and *out* of the space.

I never want you to feel trapped again.

She understood the message. On all levels. And another warm throb pulsed through her veins. Maybe Bennett was allowed into that crack. Maybe she could trust him there.

Still not willing to dwell in the deep, Hazel strode into the dimly lit room, snagged what she'd come for—a handful of orange flags she'd picked up from Mama B the last time she'd been in town—and left. Crunching through the snow, she made her way to the shooting range on the other side of the cabin, and starting at the marker where they were to take their aim, she counted strides in the opposite direction of the target. Fifteen. That should be about thirty feet, a good distance to start the penalty loop.

With a flick of her wrist, she sent a flag into the snow, pleased with herself when it stood upright. "I'll take that shot."

From there she counted on, flicking a flag into the snow every fifteen strides and moving in a wide oval around the cabin, toward the lake, and then back to the corral. Finally she reached the starting point again. She was surveying her work when an orange vehicle flashed up on the road, heading her way.

Bennett. Pleasure and pain squeezed her chest. She couldn't wait to see him again, though it'd only been a handful of days since their skiing lesson by the creek. But then she worried about seeing him again.

Would he smile at her? Would their exchanges be stilted? Where would this friendship lead them?

She knew where she wanted it to go—straight back to her in his arms, *I love yous* whispered in her ear. And she was fairly certain he hoped for the same. Hadn't he promised her that he'd always love her?

But as Little Girl Hazel had discovered long ago, not all promises got kept. Not all lost things came back.

The tires crunched on the packed snow as the little orange Bronco eased to a stop by the cabin. Before the engine was off, the passenger-side doors flew open, and both Gemma and Nathan emerged from the car.

Gemma bounced out, her normal exuberance in her step. She'd settled over the past several months, so she wasn't over the top all the time. What emerged had been a naturally positive girl, in spite of her situation. Gemma's bright personality had been a balm for Bennett and helped him transition into this guardian role he'd taken on. Hazel was grateful to the girl, for his sake.

But it was Nathan's attitude that had altered the most, and that had been within the past week. This biathlon thing had really lit something in him. Or the girl who had put him onto it. Hard to tell which for sure, but by his work and attitude the other day during their first ski session, Hazel had to believe he was really interested in the sport. No one worked that hard for a crush.

Usually.

In any case, Nathan walked toward her, erect and without a screen shoved in his face. "What are the flags for?"

She smirked at his lack of greeting. "The penalty loop. You'll have to take three trips around to meet the distance standard, but it should do the job."

"Nice." He held out a fist for her to bump. "But I won't need it."

"Cocky already."

He shook his head. "Not in me. I have the best marksman for a teacher. Bennett says so."

That seemed . . . not normal for Nathan. What was he up to?

"Are we skiing or shooting first?" Nathan didn't give her a lot of time to speculate on his sudden interest in Bennett and what she thought of his brother. Maybe he hadn't meant anything by the comment?

"We'll fire a few rounds and get a baseline of how you do at rest, then we'll see if you remember how to stay upright on skis. If you manage that, we'll see how steady your aim is with an elevated heart rate."

"A woman with a plan." Nathan smacked his gloved hands together. "I like it."

What was going on with this normally sullen kid? Hazel kept her query quiet and led the way back to the cabin. She was nearly to the steps before she caught sight of Bennett. He'd gone to the dock alone and was standing there, back to them, gaze pointed heavenward.

Heat crawled up her chest as Hazel wondered if he was listening to the sky. She shouldn't have told him.

When he turned, her heart skipped. Time and reality warped, and for a moment, Hazel thought *he's home!* As if he'd been gone on a trip and had made it back safe. Back to her.

And she wanted Elk Lake to be home for him.

Good grief. Could she be any more of a mess?

She swallowed against the growing chasm of longing as Bennett strode toward her. She shivered at the small grin that cracked his dark beard, imagining that he only ever greeted her that way. Which was silly. Bennett wasn't stingy with his smiles. Not the way she was.

"Hey, stranger." She kept casual friendliness in her tone.

"Good afternoon, Zel." He stopped next to her.

Did she imagine the twitch of his fingers or the subtle movement that made it seem that he'd reach for her hand?

Must have, because he didn't touch her. Instead, he pocketed his hand. "Thank you for making time for Nathan today."

"I'm glad to."

His blue eyes held hers for a heartbeat before he scanned the area around her cabin. "Marking a trail?"

She missed the warmth in that gaze. "Yes. For the penalty loop."

"So you'll be skiing today?"

"We'll shoot for a while first."

He nodded, his face tipped toward the ground. His jaw seemed tight. "Mind if I skip that part?"

Not surprising. Bennett still didn't like guns. Though he'd come to accept that for Hazel a gun meant something very different than for him, he wasn't comfortable around them and likely never would be. Every report of a shot made him twitch. No wonder, as he'd told Hazel he'd been a student in a school shooting. No one had died in that particular incident, but Bennett had fearful memories of being locked down in a classroom, hiding behind an overturned table out of sight line of the door's window. He could remember vividly the sounds of gunfire reverberating in the halls.

Something like that would leave a scar. Hazel could accept that.

They were so very different—she and Bennett. Came from entirely different worlds and had different outlooks on several topics. But this one they'd resolved. She didn't need to be anti-gun for him, because they were a deep-set part of her life. And he didn't need to learn to like them for her.

Sometimes differences could just be respected and left alone.

Sometimes.

All that understood, she knew Bennett didn't necessarily want to be part of Nathan's shooting practice. Hazel breached the gap between them, brushing his arm with her hand. "Of course." She turned toward the cabin. "Moose has been missing you."

Bennett's gaze found hers again, warmth in it. "Glad he's not forgotten me."

"That would never happen." Pain squeezed in her chest. She turned away from the intensity growing between them. "He's in the cabin, and there's some of that coffee you like in the cabinet. Help yourself."

Bennett nodded and then walked around her. He headed to his car, retrieved a book, and then strolled to the cabin.

"So we shoot first?" Nathan called from the deck.

"Yep." As if startled back into the present—and out of the little fantasy that the man she'd just watched go into her home had claimed as his as well. "Let's get my twenty-two and we'll see how you do."

Driven by a purpose, Hazel retrieved the weapon and a small box of ammo from the closet in her bedroom, and she quickly passed back through the cabin. Bennett made coffee at the counter, the book he'd brought waiting on the table. It was thicker than the Sherlock Holmes novels they'd spent several evenings reading together.

Ignoring the way her tummy tugged at those memories, Hazel made her way back outside. Nathan waited at the firing range.

For the next hour, they worked on his aim—both at standing and at a prone position. She had Nathan practice breathing—taking in slow, controlled breaths and exhaling quietly. He worked on finding the moment between inhale and exhale when he was perfectly still. That was the split second he needed. And he needed to find it when his heart rate was at rest and when it was elevated.

They worked on tunnel vision—shutting everything else out but the mark he wanted to hit. Not allowing sounds to distract him. Not letting activity around him to shatter the trance through which he viewed the target.

Breath in. Hold. Breath out. Hold. Breath in. Fire. Breath out.

When Nathan managed a tight pattern on the target, Hazel patted his back. "That's good."

Bright eyes—blue like his older brother's—turned to her with pride. "Yeah?"

"Yeah." She tipped her head toward the tack room. "Now let's see if you can remember how to work the skis."

Nathan's grin grew. "I'll grab them. Maybe you should tell Bennett it's time to ski? He mentioned that he wanted to try it again."

There it was again. Nathan . . . promoting Bennett? Was he trying to be a matchmaker? Or in their case, a reconciliation agent?

"You seem a lot more of a fan when it comes to your brother than you were before . . ."

Nathan shrugged, as if the comment was nothing important. "He's not so bad. As far as brothers go. Even as far as dad types go." Again he shrugged, adding as he walked away, "At least he sticks around and treats me like I can do stuff."

Ah. The conversation they'd had in the waiting room at the Big Sky hospital drifted back to mind. The one where she'd told Bennett that Nathan needed to know he could stand on his own two feet. Had she been right?

There was something both startling and satisfying in that. When had she ever been able to read people and get them?

Only with Bennett. And now with Nathan? Even Gemma? Maybe Hazel wasn't as hopelessly broken—and useless—as she'd thought. Maybe her life's purpose wasn't to stay hidden away at a mountain lake, isolated and fiercely independent.

Strange, she'd not thought that was a bad purpose before. But now . . .

These people—the Croftons and Hunter and Janie. And Mama B and even Tara. They mattered to her, more than she ever thought possible. She *needed* them—and maybe they needed her, and maybe that wasn't a dangerously bad thing after all.

Life just got bigger. And like the deep, starry sky on a clear, moonless night, the lure of complex beauty seemed undeniably compelling.

***

Bennett's heart rate thumbed at a steady, elevated rhythm. This Nordic skiing thing had some distinct advantages over an expensive treadmill in a high-rise workout room. The first of which were the clean, crisp air and the near-blinding bright beauty of a pristine winter scene. White glittered in every direction, a million sparkles set off by the late-afternoon sun, interrupted only by evergreen trees and patches of exposed granite too steep to hold snow on their faces.

And the second advantage? Sharing this exhilarating workout with Hazel and Nathan—made even richer by watching the pair bring out the best in each other.

A gift. That was what these moments were. A gift that not so long ago the old Bennett Crofton would have considered an inconvenience, if not a burden. Praise God for grace that not only had saved his soul but was at work changing his life.

Would Hazel ever know this wonder for herself? *Please, God, let it be so.*

As he leaned against the ski poles, white puffs of air billowing from his elevated breath, Bennett watched Hazel and Nathan at the start of the penalty loop she'd marked out. Together the three of them had already done a half dozen laps. Good enough of a workout for Bennett. His calf muscles burned and quads quivered a touch. But Nathan wasn't done, and Hazel had more than enough left in her to match his endurance. With a "ready, go" from Hazel, the two shot off again. Nathan moved remarkably well on his skis, considering this was only his second outing.

Had he ever thought about running cross-country at his school in Chicago? By this show of stamina, he'd likely be good at it.

Hazel easily kept pace with him, her experience and long-earned elevation acclamation working to her advantage. But it didn't look like she was holding back for Nathan's sake. Given a little more time and conditioning, Nathan would likely take her. And by Hazel's eager investment in him, she'd cheer him on when he did so.

Hazel was blossoming before Bennett's eyes. He'd already loved her, and that wasn't going to change. But to see her become more—this selfless, giving, encouraging woman where there had been shadows of a self-consumed girl—it only made the fondness for her grow. And with that grew the aching hope that she'd know and understand love. Real love—from the ultimate source.

Don't stop with singing stars, Lord. Show her who You are.

As Bennett whispered that prayer, he thought of the Bible he'd left on her kitchen table and the note he'd tucked within. He hadn't known what to write, exactly. He'd already told her about his faith—about Jesus dying for sins and being saved by faith in Him. Hazel hadn't cared to listen.

But he sensed she was listening now—and not necessarily to him. So he'd penned a small note, the words seeming inadequate, and prayed that the Word of God would find root in the emerging cracks of her armored heart. That seemed all he could do, because while he'd been given the privilege to share truth with the woman he loved, he wasn't the one who could save her.

He wondered if this combination of agony and hope had resided with his mom all those years that he had wandered down a path of selfish destruction. Likely so. He'd apologize to her again. And thank her for her faithful prayers on his behalf.

Man, that was a legacy he could grab on to. One of faithfulness. One that could maybe, by God's hand, alter the trajectory of not only his life but those who came after him. He didn't have to walk his father's path. Nor did Nathan and Gemma.

And Hazel?

She would have to choose for herself. But he'd do as his mother had done.

Pray.

CHAPTER NINETEEN

HAZEL WONDERED AT THE sting of tears in her eyes. She wasn't the crying type. Especially at something like this.

A note tucked into a Bible.

When had she ever been interested in a Bible? But there it sat, open on the thick comforter spread over her lap. She was propped up against a pair of stacked pillows, dressed in her flannel pj bottoms and a long-sleeve thermal top, hot tea at her bedside table. All ready to call it a day.

Usually she'd reach over to the bedside lamp, snap it off, and lose herself to the oblivion of sleep. Except that hadn't happened quite so smoothly lately. In the past several weeks, actually. Instead she'd lie there and wonder why she couldn't commit to a man she deeply loved. Why couldn't she let go of the fear? And why had she felt compelled, multiple times, to go to the Black Gulch, only to come back with that same cold, ugly feeling?

Why did her world feel so out of control?

And now more recently, why did the sky sing?

She had spiraled into madness.

Except now she held a Bible on her lap and a note scrawled in Bennett's penmanship. Not a love note but one that gripped her heart all the same.

I believe God is willing and able to employ extraordinary measures to reach ordinary people. He calls to our lost souls in a way we can't deny. We can choose to ignore it, but that choice doesn't invalidate the offer. The invitation.

I offer myself as your first exhibit. Who else but God alone could coordinate a spoiled city boy to lose his memory in the wild mountains of Montana so that he would remember the God of his childhood? That is an extraordinary tale, don't you think? I am humbled that God would pursue me with such tenacity.

I told you I didn't believe you were losing your mind. Instead, perhaps you're finding something. Maybe it would be more correct to say that you've been offered something. A glimpse of a heavenly anthem of praise, music that cries out the glory of God.

You believe in what you can see and hear and touch. God is inviting you to see and hear His glory. It is a royal invitation, Hazel. One you alone can decide what to do with. But may I point you to a few verses I have recently come across in my daily reading? I've marked them in this Bible, a gift of love I pass on to you.

Keep listening, Hazel. It is Love that pursues your soul.

Rather than signing his name, Bennett had left two lines at the bottom of the page. One read *Psalm 34:8*. The other, *Psalm 95:7–8*.

That was all. Confusing. Compelling.

Hazel shifted her burning gaze back to the open Bible and read the part that Bennett had highlighted in Psalm 95.

If you hear His voice, do not harden your hearts . . .

What was the context? What was this writer referencing in the following parts—*as at Meribah, as on the day at Massah in the wilderness, when your fathers put me to the test and put me to the proof, though they had seen my work . . .*

Hazel felt lost but driven as she considered these strange words referencing a foreign story. Reaching for her laptop on the other side of the bed, she opened the screen, waited for Chrome to load, typed in the words, and opened the first hyperlink the search provided. The article pointed her to another book in the Bible—to Leviticus. She read the story, and it left more questions than answers.

Water? From a stone in the desert? Crazy. Who believed this kind of thing?

She let the Bible drop from her hands, landing back on her lap. As if something prompted her to do so, her attention drifted to the window on the other side of the room.

Stars sparkled against the velvet black sky.

Had she truly heard them sing? That was crazy.

Who would believe that sort of thing?

Bennett did. Hunter might. Janie. Mama B—

Mama B. That was who Hazel should talk to.

CHAPTER TWENTY

"BENNETT, YOU'VE TAKEN TO Luna like a moose in a creek."

Bennett eyed Mama B, wondering if she meant to bring up how he'd lost his memory to a moose before he'd lost his heart to a mountain woman.

With a cackle and a smack on the front counter, Mama B winked. "How appropriate was that?"

"Thoroughly," he said drily.

"A laugh a day, my boy. A laugh a day."

"What does a laugh a day do?"

"Keeps the winter depression away."

"Is that how that works?"

She shrugged. "Most years. Though I'll own to knowing some pretty dark seasons."

Nodding, Bennett wondered if Mama B had seen some dark days recently. Wouldn't blame her one bit, having found out the guy who'd run out on his wife and daughter had a whole other secret family down South. He knew exactly how that felt.

He leaned his hip against the counter and crossed his arms. "You doing okay, MB?"

Mama B met his steady look, held it for a serious moment, and nodded. "I am, Bennett. Thank you for caring though. Mike and I ended a long time ago, and I have to believe that God brought Livy into our lives for a reason. Just like he brought you."

Bennett nodded. Life in Luna seemed to be like a large puzzle with tiny, intricate pieces. The full picture was yet to be seen, but as little sections fit together, things started to make more sense.

That did beg the question, though: Were he and Hazel ever going to fit together?

"What brings you in today?" Mama B redirected their visit to business.

"A ski suit. Or uniform. Or whatever it might be called."

"For Nathan?"

"Right. He has a competition in mind, and I'd like to surprise him with something that won't make him feel like an outsider."

Mama nodded with approval. "Let's check my catalog and see what we can find." She turned, snatched her laptop, and brought it to the counter between them. With a few clicks, she had a site up with cross-country ski gear on the page.

They spent several minutes discussing trousers, gilets, jerseys, and headgear, as well as Nathan's favorite colors. As far as Bennett could tell, black and gray. Once all was picked out, Mama B sent in the order, and Bennett paid the bill.

"I was thinking about you the other day, Bennett." Mama handed back his card. "While I was doing my Bible reading."

"Were you?" How was this going to go? Heaven knew he'd made enough mistakes in the past year alone to earn himself a long sermon.

Mama smiled, warmth lighting her blue eyes. "Indeed I was. I was reading First Corinthians thirteen. You know—the love chapter?"

He nodded. He was familiar with that—mostly because of the handful of weddings he'd attended. Had Mama B weddings on her mind? Maybe—but she should probably keep her thoughts on that score aimed at Janie and Hunter. After all, they were actually engaged. Not that Bennett didn't wish he were too.

But that wasn't where he was in life right then. At the moment it didn't seem likely he ever would be.

"I was reading through those old familiar words, and it dawned on me." Mama B reached below the counter, pulled up her worn copy of the Holy Word, and used a ribbon to flip open the thin pages. With her finger, she traced down, stopping at the passage she wanted, and then began reading aloud. Except, her recitation was a little altered. "Bennett is patient. Bennett is kind. Bennett doesn't envy. He isn't puffed up, he does not behave rudely . . ."

Heat flared up his neck and washed over his face. While MB continued to read, inserting his name in that well-known and impossible-to-live-up-to passage, he looked down at his shoes as steamy liquid pricked his eyes.

He was not that man. Not even close.

A small, work-callused hand covered his, still resting on the counter, and then Mama B finished softly. "Bennett will endure this thing."

Pressing his lips tight, Bennett struggled for control. "I don't think I deserve such praise." He lifted his gaze to meet Mama's kind look. "If you remember who I was when I first came to town—"

"That old man is gone. The new stands before me now."

"And if you knew how much I've already screwed up things with Hazel—"

"Bennett, I know." Her soft claim carried the weight of truth. Of course she knew. She'd been here all those times he'd stayed with

Hazel. She wasn't ignorant. "I'm not saying you're a perfect man. No man is. What I am saying is that I see what you are straining to become—and the work of Christ in you. It is a thing to behold, and I'm honored to have a front-row view." That rough hand squeezed his. "And this friendship you are pursuing with Hazel . . . I think it's wise. I'm sure it's hard when I know that you love her and want things to be different between you right now. But it is a selfless love that would lay down your own desires to seek what is best for her."

Her stout praise ironically stirred up doubt in his heart. It didn't matter what he did or didn't do, how much he wanted her to know the wholeness he'd found in Jesus. Hazel would have to choose for herself. "Do you think she'll ever understand the void she feels will only be filled by the One who made her soul?"

Mama B held a half smile—one that wasn't entirely promising but still hopeful. "I think that you and me, Hunter and Janie, your mom—and so many others that I know or know of—are walking miracles. Every redemption story, no matter how big or small they seem, are miracles. And I think we should hope for the same for Hazel. Hope, and not give up."

As he drove the winding narrow road toward the Splendor, Bennett couldn't get the conversation with Mama B from his mind. Had he hoped the way that love should? Lately, it seemed like he felt that hope slip away a little more each day.

Or maybe he'd confused the hope for Hazel's eternal salvation with the hope he still held out for *them*. He needed to sort that out, get it straight. Her eternity was significantly more important than his longing for marital bliss. If he'd gotten that straight in the first place, maybe they wouldn't be in the mess they'd tumbled into now.

Even so, there had been good despite his failures. He didn't regret moving there, for example. And if he hadn't moved, he wasn't sure he'd have taken in his siblings—and he had to admit, he was glad he had.

Huh. There was that—a huge thing. He'd come to know and love Nathan and Gemma in a way that wasn't possible before. They had a real relationship—one that made it difficult to imagine life after they went back to Chicago.

He pushed that dreary thought away. Not something he needed to wrestle with right then.

The point was that even though he'd made some big mistakes with Hazel, there had been enormous blessings on this twisted path. Friendships like he'd never had before. People who studied the Word with him and prayed with him and encouraged him. God was working for good, in spite of Bennett's mistakes.

Please work for her good too.

His prayer lifted from his heart as he parked beside the lodge. From outside appearances, the large log structure was complete. Inside, he knew there were still a few larger projects to finish—the bathrooms and the kitchen being the biggest of those. But even if they didn't get completed by the May deadline, now just three weeks away, the wedding would go on.

Bennett grinned as he stomped his feet on the thick welcome mat before he entered the front door. Hunter and Janie were good together, and it was nice to see them happy.

The heavy door swung open in front of him, Hunter waiting on the other side. "Hey, bruh. Come in."

"Thanks." Bennett kicked off his shoes beside the pair of Muk boots in the entry. "Think the snow will be completely gone by your wedding day?"

Hunter shrugged, leading the way to the back office. "Maybe. Up here you never know. We could get a three-foot dumping after a week of fifty degrees and sunshine." He walked around the large desk that had arrived last week. Several stacks of papers, a pair of large envelopes, and his laptop sat on the surface.

Hunter sat on the folding chair behind the desk and grinned. "Either way, though, we're getting married. That's all I care about."

Bennett chuckled. "I can understand that." He gestured toward the scattered paperwork. "This why you asked me to come up?"

"Yeah." Hunter reached for the pile to his left, thumbed through the pages, then held them up to Bennett. "This is the advertising proposal I'm leaning toward. But I wanted your opinion before I commit."

Bennett accepted the pages with a nod. "Sure. Do you have anything I can compare it with?"

One finger in the air, Hunter scanned the other stacks. Then he selected two. "These."

"Good. Mind if I take them home to look them over?"

"Sure." Hunter leaned back, a look of hesitation crossing his bearded face. "Take the week. Janie and I are going out of town anyway."

"Out of town?" Bennett helped himself to a large mailer and slipped the ad proposals inside.

Hunter rubbed the back of his head. "Yeah. Not the greatest timing, I know. But Livy needs to get home, and we aren't keen on her driving by herself."

"I see." Bennett nodded. "Anything I can do for you here, while you're gone?"

"Check on the progress up here?"

Another nod.

"And my sister?"

His gut twinged. A few months ago, Hunter wouldn't have even asked. He wouldn't have felt the need to. Even so, Bennett held a steady look. "Of course."

CHAPTER
TWENTY-ONE

TRAFFIC FLOWED AT A steady clip as Hunter drove Livy's Ford Focus south past the Wyoming-Colorado border. The Rocky Mountains emerged to the west where, through much of Wyoming, there'd been a wide spread of windy plains. They would follow that rise of rolling purple peaks all the way through the I-25 corridor of Colorado.

Hunter blew out a breath, his backside sore. They still had a long way to go, and he was not used to sitting in a car for hours on end.

"Having regrets?" Janie reached across the small space between their seats.

Hunter took her fingers and wove them with his. "About this trip? No. I'm glad we get to do this together, and I'm relieved Livy's not taking this trip alone again. That was on the crazy side for her to do it in the first place."

Janie chuckled. "She's determined."

"Like her big sister."

A steady quiet, underscored by the rhythmic humming of the tires rolling at seventy-five miles per hour on the pavement, settled between them. Hunter's mind traveled back to Montana and back to the topic that had unsettled his rest over the past week. He glanced back at Livy. The girl was curled up against her pillow, which was jammed against the window, snuggled beneath one of Janie's fluffy gray blankets, and as he'd suspected, sound asleep.

"Something else is on your mind?" Janie said.

Hunter returned his attention to the road.

"About Livy?"

"No. But there is something I wanted to talk with you about."

"That sounds . . . ominous." Janie glanced toward the backseat as well. "Is it something private?"

"Not really. Just . . . sensitive."

"Isn't that the same thing?"

"No. I don't mean that I don't want Livy to hear. I mean that you might not appreciate what I'm considering. In fact, I'm pretty sure you won't like it at all."

"Hmm. You make me sound . . . controlling. Or narrow minded."

Hunter squeezed her hand. "I don't think either of those things about you."

"How about you tell me, and I promise to hear you out?"

"That's what I'd hoped for." He released her hand, gripped the steering wheel with both hands, and searched for a place to start.

"You remember when I told you last week that José had something hard going on in his life that he shared with our men's group?"

"Yeah . . . You said he was pretty upset about something out of his control."

"Right."

"And you want to help him?"

"If I—if *we*—can. I feel like we should. Like God is asking us to be willing, at least."

"Okay. Want to tell me what we're going to be willing to do?"

Hunter swallowed. Shot up a prayer for guidance—and *please don't let this turn into a fight.* Then he met Janie's gaze with a side glance. "It's Isa."

"Isa?" A hesitant frown carried through her voice. "What about Isa?"

"First, let's just be honest about something here, okay? Last fall, at the groundbreaking party, she didn't know there had ever been anything between you and me. She didn't mean to stir up trouble."

Janie sat still. And silent.

Hunter reached for her hand again. "I was the jerk. It wasn't Isa's fault. She might be on the flirty side of friendly, but she truly had no idea what was going on beneath the surface between you and me. Not any more than Grady did."

After several throbbing heartbeats, Janie squeezed his fingers again and nodded. "Okay. I can see that. So you're asking me not to hold that night against Isa?"

"Right."

"And you don't hold a grudge against Grady?"

"No. And I hope he doesn't hold me in contempt either. It was our fault, you know? Mostly mine. If we could have worked things out, figured out how to be honest without dragging other people into our drama, it would have been better for everyone."

"I can agree to that."

Hunter exhaled, relief unwinding in his gut.

"So what's going on with Isa?"

"José is really worried about her—she's gotten herself into some-thing that isn't good."

"Something such as . . ."

"A man."

"I take it he's not one José approves of?"

Hunter nodded.

"Does he have good reason for his disapproval?"

"For starters, the guy is married."

"Yikes."

"Yeah. But that wasn't his first concern—he didn't know that little fact until he did some digging. Isa has basically cut them off. All the Romeros. Why would she do that? Why would she turn her back on her family when they love her so much, you know?"

Janie listened, and Hunter caught her nod in his periphery. "That sounds suspicious," she said.

"Right. So José did some digging—and obviously didn't like what he found. He confronted Isa about it in a text, and she sent him a terse *mind your own business* response and hasn't responded to any of his calls or texts since. He's pretty sure she's blocked his number."

"Wow." Janie sighed. "That's really awful. The Romeros must be pretty torn up about it."

"Yeah. They are. José was close to tears when he told us."

Leaning close, Janie rubbed Hunter's shoulder. "I love this ten-derheartedness of yours, Hunt."

He pressed a quick kiss into her hair.

"But I don't see how we can help," she continued. "I mean, if she won't even talk to José, how are we going to reach her?"

"I don't know." Hunter's shoulders drooped. "All I know is that I feel this prompting to be available."

"Available for what?"

"To be a safe place for her to land, if that's what is needed." He met her eyes again, daring to hold the gaze for more than a split second.

There was hesitation there.

"You mean for her to come stay with us?"

"For her to come to Luna . . ."

"And what would she do in Luna?"

He clenched his jaw, aware that this could be the end of their peaceful conversation. Sharing with Janie about Isa's trouble was one thing. This though—this might be crossing the line.

"You want me to take her on at the café, don't you?"

Hunter squirmed. "Maybe it would be a good thing for both of you? I mean, once the lodge is up and running, you'll need help. You said so yourself."

Silence met his response. A long, tight silence.

Then, "Were you thinking she'd move into my apartment too?"

Yeah, he had, actually. Once they were married, at least. Then Janie would be living with him at the lodge. What had she planned to do with the space above the café? "Janie . . ." He felt defeated and frustrated and foolish all at once. He knew he didn't have any ground to be offering up Janie's stuff—employment or living quarters. Particularly to a young woman who had proven herself to be more than, as he'd just put it, on the flirty side of friendly.

Isa could be trouble. A whole heap of trouble.

But surely by now Janie knew she owned Hunter's whole heart, didn't she? Certainly she understood there was no risk where that was concerned.

Janie's long sigh filled the tense silence. "I can see what you're saying."

"But you're not for it."

"I didn't say that."

She didn't have to.

Her arm curled around his elbow. "Can we think about it for a while?"

"Of course. As you pointed out, Isa's not talking to her family right now anyway." The yucky weight in his chest lightened. She wasn't livid. It wasn't a hard *no* and *what are you thinking?* "I think we should pray about it. Together."

"Hmm."

There was a smile. One that sent a warm thrill through his heart. Look at them, working through an issue like adults who loved each other.

"I like that—together." She snuggled into his arm. "We'll pray for Isa. Together."

CHAPTER
TWENTY-TWO

SHE WOKE UP TO sinus pressure in her head and what felt like a
weight on her chest.

Hazel groaned as she rolled from her back to her side. The thick
covers she usually hoarded around her shoulders these cold winter
mornings had been kicked to the end of the bed. She still felt hot.
Wiggling her aching body, she sat up enough to peel her long-sleeve

thermal off and then dropped back against the mattress in her tank top.

She was sick.

It'd been forever since she'd been sick. Like, the last time she could remember, she'd been in high school. She never got sick. Might be because she'd had extremely limited human contact up until this past year.

By the sharp pains flashing in her back, and the deep, dull ache in every other muscle of her body, she was in for a doozy. She wasn't prepared to be sick. No cold medicine. Hazel didn't even keep acetaminophen on hand—something Bennett had noted the first time he'd come to the cabin as her boyfriend last year. He'd had an altitude headache, and she had nothing for it. He'd gone to town and bought a small bottle of ibuprofen.

Had he left it there, along with the coffee he preferred?

A deep, rattling cough racked through her chest, so fierce her eyes watered.

Chamomile tea. That was what she needed—and knew she had that in the cupboard. She just needed to heat some water and probably get a fire going in the fireplace so the cabin would stay decently warm.

Dragging herself out of bed, she moaned again. From her corner of the room, Scout popped up from her rag-rug bed. The dog's wagging tail quickly drooped as she observed Hazel's stooped shuffle from the bedroom. Trotting beside her, Scout let out a soft whine.

You okay?

"I'll live, girl." Hazel coughed again, dropping into a kitchen chair. Then she sniffed, leaned down to Scout's head, which rested on her leg, and pressed her forehead against the dog's soft fur. "I think."

It was like all the years of not getting sick were now going to bite her in the backside.

Scout whined again, then licked Hazel's cheek.

"Yuck." Hazel forced herself to sit up. "You're not supposed to do that, and you know it."

The dog's head dropped from her leg. *Sorry.* With a quick peek back up at her, she pivoted and ran to the large quilt by the window, where the other three dogs lay. She nosed Moose, who lifted his head, and then Scout let out a short yip. *Something's wrong with Mom!*

Moose looked at Hazel.

"I'm fine." Hazel waved the old man down, to tell him not to get up for her. "Just a cold." Her palms pressed against the table, she levered herself up to stand and then shuffled to get the water going. "Man, though. My head feels like it might rupture, and I think you rolled over me a few times while I slept last night."

Scout trotted back to her, spun a circle, and then sat.

"Right. You need to go out."

At the word *out*, Ice and Cream were on their feet and at the front door. Hazel opened it, and the three younger dogs shot out. Moose lumbered Hazel's way, but instead of going straight out, he paused beside her and pressed his weight into her leg.

"I'll be okay, boy."

He looked up, licked her hand, then walked out the door.

The frosty morning air had felt good on her burning skin just a moment ago, but now a chill fell over her shoulders. A violent shiver had her shutting the door and turning for her room to retrieve the warmer shirt she'd only just shed.

Long sleeves back in place, and her grandmother's sweater applied for good measure, Hazel wandered back to the kitchen, waited for the teapot to whistle, and made herself a cup of chamomile tea. And yes, there in the cabinet, next to Bennett's coffee, was a small bottle of medicine.

"Thanks, Benji." Hazel took two and then collapsed onto the couch. After another coughing fit, a tear leaked onto her cheek. She was too tired to deny that it came from missing that man just as much as it had been forced by the cough.

The sun shone brilliantly against the melting ice covering Elk Lake. Bennett tugged on the brim of his hat, shielding his eyes from the blinding white as he scanned the area in front of Hazel's cabin. Snow still blanketed most of the land, though the trails had melted into a muddy brown.

It was lovely and quiet. Too quiet, actually. Sliding up his coat sleeve, Bennett turned his wrist to check his watch. Nearly ten thirty. Zel was usually out doing chores at this hour. Unless she'd gone on some trek? There was that possibility.

But something seemed off.

"Zel?" Bennett called as he stepped onto one of those melted paths and wound his way to the front of the cabin. A trio of heads popped out from under the front deck near the steps, followed quickly by a round of yips.

"Hey, guys." Bennett stopped to pet each furry head as they danced at his feet. If the dogs were all there, Hazel hadn't gone anywhere. He looked up at the cabin, noting that the chimney lacked the typical stream of gray smoke.

He looked back down at Scout. "Where is she, hmm?"

The pup took off up the steps and sat on the deck beside the front door. There she looked back at Bennett and whined.

Something was definitely off.

Kicking his boots off first, Bennett tapped on the front door, then opened it. "Zel?"

He stepped inside, and the dogs all clambered in after him. Man, it was chilly in there. He could see his breath. Not that Hazel kept her cabin on the toasty side of warm, but she usually kept it comfortable enough not to need gloves.

"Hazel?"

Moose appeared, his big head poking around the sofa, and let out a soft bark. It wasn't the *hi* sort of sound Bennett usually got from the old man, and the dog didn't lumber his way over to greet him. Instead, he looked back at the sofa and whined.

Bennett understood. With a few quick strides, he found Hazel. Curled up in a ball on the couch, pale as the melting snow and hot to the touch. He went down on one knee and pressed his cold palm to her fiery forehead. "Hazel."

One rattling breath lifted her lungs, and she moaned on the exhale, but she didn't open her eyes.

Heart kicking into high gear, Bennett cupped her face in both hands. "Hazel, honey. Wake up."

"Ben . . ." she wheezed.

"Yeah, I'm here. Can you look at me?"

"Hurts."

"What hurts?" He moved his hands to her shoulders, then to her hands. Her fingers were like ice.

"Chest."

"Your chest hurts?"

"Head."

"Both?"

"Everything."

He held her hands in one of his own, hoping to warm those fingers, and moved to feel her head again with the other hand. Man, she was really hot.

"Oh, Zel, I think you have the flu."

It had been going around in town. Several kids at school had missed, according to Gemma. Nathan hadn't felt the best last week, but whatever he'd had was nothing like this.

Bennett stood, taking inventory of the dark cabin. No fire. He'd build one. After he tucked a blanket around Hazel and started some water for tea. Then he'd call his mom and ask her what else he should do.

Pivoting on his socked foot, he walked to her room and found her bed unmade—very much not typical for Hazel. She was a neat-and-tidy checklist kind of woman. Bennett grabbed the thick blue blanket that was clumped at the end of her bed.

He'd given her that blanket. Bought it in Jackson, Wyoming, when he'd flown that route on one of his visits last winter. He swallowed hard as the memory of them snuggled together beneath it melted in his mind. He gripped the blanket as a rebellious wish for those intimate moments stole through his thoughts.

In so many ways, it would have been easier to have simply carried on as they had been.

If he could have swallowed the guilt he'd felt every time they'd made love, blocked out the whispered accusation, *She is not your wife.* And ignored the sting of responsibility every time his conscious told him he was failing her soul.

Would they be happy, right now, if he'd not changed course? She wouldn't have woken alone with the flu and lay in a frigid cabin by herself for who knew how long.

But he would not be making strides toward becoming the man he wanted to be. No, he'd be more like the man he'd been before. The one Hazel had despised. The one *he* had despised.

Why did this battle still rage?

He'd surrendered to God, done what he believed he was supposed to. Had confessed the sin of his flesh, repented, and turned away. Prayed for Hazel's soul and for the redemption of their relationship.

And yet there he stood, wishing back that which he should have never taken in the first place.

Mama B's gentle voice intruded upon his war. *Bennett hopes all things . . . He will endure this thing.*

If MB could see this battle within him right now, would she say such nice things—implying that he, a man who constantly struggled with sin, was a godly man?

Frustration and shame seeped into his heart, cooling the fire that had stirred there. Shaking his head, he turned and left her room, focusing his mind on what was real and needed right now. Hazel was sick, and she needed him to take care of her.

Snagging a pillow, he retreated from the room and made his way back to Hazel. Kneeling beside her, he helped her sit up enough to tuck the pillow behind her, then gently snugged the blanket around her frame.

Her skin was cool to the touch now.

"You're shivering," he said.

"Hmm."

"I'll make you some tea." Then he was on his feet and hustling to get the job started. Once the teakettle was on the stove, he worked on the fire. The smoldering ashes within the stove indicated she had started one at some point that morning. It must have been a while ago though. That likely meant that she'd not gotten any of the chores done.

After a few minutes, Bennett coaxed a small flame to life. He stood and surveyed the dogs. "Have you been fed?"

Ice and Cream popped off their blanket and went straight for the door. Moose eased himself up from the spot he'd claimed on the floor in front of the sofa. Only Scout remained sitting, her chin resting on the sofa cushion beside Hazel's feet.

"She'll be okay, pup." Bennett stopped to scratch Scout's head and then went to the door. "Let's go eat, and then you can come back and keep watch."

Scout eyed Bennett, then turned to look at Moose. The big dog walked toward the front door, his exit inspiring Scout to come along as well.

It took nearly twenty minutes to get the work done that Bennett could remember. Dogs fed. Horses fed. Water brought up from the lake—after the ice was broken near the dock. Wood stacked near the front door replenished from the larger stack back by the tack room. Once he was done, Scout and Moose were ready to go back inside.

By the time Bennett brought Hazel a mug of tea, she'd tossed the blanket off her shoulders. The shivering was gone, replace by beads of sweat along her brow. He sat on the edge of a cushion near her hip and felt her cheek with the back of his hand.

"Burning hot again," he said. "Would you rather have a cold glass of water?"

She nodded. "I wasn't sure you were actually here."

"What?"

"I thought maybe I'd imagined it."

He chuckled and went back to the kitchen. "I'm here. Was just outside taking care of the animals."

"Thank you." She accepted his help to sit up and then sipped the cold water. "What time is it?"

"Almost eleven."

Hazel shook her head. "Good thing you came. Poor horses were probably panicked."

"They seemed happy to see me."

She sipped again and then laid a timid hand on his arm. "How did you know?"

"That the animals needed fed?"

"That I needed you?" Her glassy eyes met his, and so much more was said in that look than in those four simple words.

Bennett wanted to gather her close and hold her. Whisper promises that he'd always be there, whether she needed him or not. Call an end to this friend zone he'd put them in.

With clenched fists, he instead forced a tight smile. "I came up to tell you about a competition Nathan wants to enter."

Hazel looked down, and her fingers drifted away from his arm. "Oh."

"I'm glad I did. You're pretty sick, Zel." He took the glass of water from her hand.

She lay back and shut her eyes. "I don't feel great, that's for sure."

He could no longer deny the need to touch her. He fingered her hair, then smoothed it away from her fevered brow. "I'm here now."

Her chest rose and fell with a wheezing breath, then she covered his hand with her own. Pressing her face into his palm, she sighed. "I'm glad."

And then she fell asleep.

CHAPTER
TWENTY-THREE

"DAD SAYS HE WANTS to see you."

Janie froze, the shirt she'd just folded to pack into her bag becoming a crumpled mess in her fist. She lifted her head and then turned to the door behind her, where Livy had just fired that missile from.

"What?"

Livy bit her bottom lip, her gaze aimed at Janie's feet. "I talked to him today—Mom said I had to tell him what I did." She stuffed her hands into her mom-jeans pockets and crossed her bare feet. "I don't know why"—she shrugged, then raised her eyes to meet Janie's—"but when I told him that I found you and that you and Hunter brought me home, he said he'd like to see you again."

Nope. Absolutely not. Janie wasn't willing to stretch that far.

Hunter appeared in the hall behind Livy, his cautious look telling Janie that he'd overheard. One hand on Livy's shoulder, he continued to look at Janie. "Liv, how about you give Janie and me a minute?"

Livy looked up at Hunter, her expression a mask of miserable apology. "I didn't mean to make so much trouble for you guys."

"There's been no trouble," Hunter said. "Just things to process. Your mom said something about Torchy Tacos."

A smile chased away Livy's frown. She looked at Janie. "You have to try the Tipsy Chick."

Janie attempted a grin. "If you say so. As long as there isn't any fish in it."

"No fish. Got it." Livy turned her attention to Hunter. "I think you'd like the Chili Wagon. That's what my boyfriend always gets."

"I'll trust you on that." Hunter stepped back, a silent invitation for Livy to vacate the area.

The girl took the hint and made her way toward the main living area of the house—one that was on the upper end of middle class. Four bedrooms, three baths, spacious kitchen, and large living area. Not what Janie had imagined when Livy had told her that not only their dad was an alcoholic, but her mom should be in rehab.

The last part an outright lie.

Bethany Fraser Truitt was a lovely woman. One who had been born and raised in Austin and had fallen in love with a man who'd landed in her life at twenty-nine.

"He was a wounded, lost soul," Bethany had said of Mike. "Carrying a whole load of regret. And I was tenderhearted and believed him when he said he wanted a fresh chance at a clean life. He did try."

Janie had asked if Bethany had ever known about her and her mother.

Bethany nodded, but then shook her head. "Mike said that there was no space for reconciliation. I assumed that meant that he'd been told to leave and never come back." She sighed. "It made me all the more defensive of him—that he'd been banished from his own home, his own daughter."

It had been hard to keep her temper in check. Hunter's strong hand holding hers helped, but even so, Janie nearly lost it.

Until Bethany added, "I don't doubt your side of the story, Janie. And I'm sorry for it. Mike does try, when he's sober, to be a better man. But he has never been able to take responsibility for his mistakes—which might be why he can't stay sober. There's always an excuse."

At that point, Janie had wondered why Bethany was still married to the man. But that wasn't her business. They were there to deliver Livy safely home—to a mother who clearly cared about her daughter. Janie and Hunter stayed overnight as guests and had arranged a flight into Bozeman the next day.

The sound of the door clicking shut jarred Janie back into the present. Lowering the now-rumpled shirt into her travel bag, she shook her head. "I'm not going to—"

"Janie." Hunter's hands warmed Janie's arms as he turned her toward him.

"Don't, Hunt."

"You'll always wonder."

Tears pricked her eyes. "No I won't."

"This has been eating you for as long as I've known you. Go." He cupped her cheek with one hand, tracing her cheekbone with the pad of his thumb. "Face him."

She shook her head. "He doesn't deserve . . ." The swelling of her throat cut off the words.

"I'll be there with you."

"It won't matter. I don't want to see him."

Hunter's lips seamed, but his steady look told her he wasn't willing to let this go.

"You don't understand what it's like to discover your dad just ditched you to go have a whole other family. Lied about you—saying that you rejected him. He rejected us, Hunt!"

His slow nod accompanied the filling of compassion in his eyes. "I know. But, Janie? I know what it's like not to have a dad at all. And I also know what it's like to lose someone to alcohol, never having reconciled the past. It doesn't all just die with them, hon. It doesn't just go away."

"But it was *their* choice!"

"You're right. This one, though, is yours. I just don't want you adding regret to resentment."

The lighting was soft yellow, glowing gently against the light-sage walls. The deep-blue furniture played a nice contrast to the paint color. Things Janie took note of by way of distraction—but that wasn't very successful.

Her core trembled as she sat in the small visiting room. Even with Hunter's fingers laced with hers, she felt vulnerable and terrified.

God, I don't want to do this!

But it was too late, and though he wouldn't have forced her, ultimately Hunter would have been disappointed in her if she hadn't consented to meeting Mike. Or maybe he would have been disappointed *for* her. She was too distraught to tease out the difference.

The door swung open. Janie sucked in a breath. She and Hunter both stood.

"Mr. Truitt." The attendant—or whatever the person's title was—swept a hand toward the little sitting area. "You'll have fifteen minutes." Then the woman swept out of the room.

A chill settled in the room as the door clicked shut. Mike Truitt stood unmoving. He had dark hair, salted generously with silver, and blue eyes.

Like Janie.

She trembled as Mike's gaze met hers.

"Is that my little Jumping Jane?"

Her spine stiffened as she swallowed. She'd forgotten that nickname. Only her dad had ever used it.

"Janie," she said stiffly.

Hunter's arm slipped around her as Mike walked closer.

The man looked down, then back up into Janie's face. "My long-lost daughter. Do you have a hug for your daddy?"

Janie closed her lips in a flat line. She felt Hunter's arm around her tighten.

"I'm Hunter Wallace."

"Wallace . . ." Mike looked up and to the right, as if accessing memory from long past. "From up at the lake?"

"Yes."

"You grew up."

"I did. We both did."

"I see that." Giving up on the hug Janie was clearly not willing to give, Mike backed to a chair and lowered onto it.

A long, unsettling silence snaked between the trio. Mike cleared his throat and leaned his elbows onto his knees. "I take it you weren't ready for a family reunion." He looked up at Janie.

"I didn't even know you were still alive until Olivia showed up in my café telling me we were sisters."

He nodded. "I should have reached out a long time ago."

"But you didn't."

He looked down at the floor. "A mistake."

"Seems you've made more than your fair share of those," Janie said.

Hunter squeezed her elbow.

Mike cleared his throat. "Yes. I guess that's true."

"You guess?" Janie sat forward. Never mind everything with herself and her mom. How about the perpetual chaos he put his current family in now? "Livy says this is your third time in rehab."

Warm color seeped into Mikes face, a pink contrast to his dark five o'clock shadow. "Didn't know she kept track."

"How could she not?" Janie's voice rose. "How could you think that what you do doesn't affect other people? Your *daughter*?"

"She and her mother have a nice house. Livy keeps busy at school. She's doing fine."

"She drove over a thousand miles in the dead of winter to Montana to find me. Does that sound like she's doing fine?"

He hung his head.

"Look. I'm grown up now, and what's done is done. It can't be taken back. Livy though? She's still a kid. She still clings to hope that her dad is going to figure out how to be a decent father. Don't wreck her life."

As Mike lifted his face, regret filled his expression. "Like I did yours?"

Janie felt Hunter watching her. She drew in a deep breath, trying to clear the clutter of anger and hurt from her mind. What mattered now was Livy. Slowly, as Janie exhaled, she shook her head. "You know what? I'm okay. Mama and me, we did okay, in spite of your abandonment."

Mike nodded.

"Are you willing to risk a different outcome with Livy?"

He sat back and sighed. "I think sometimes she'd be better off without me." He shot a stabbing look her way. "Seems you were."

"Nice, Dad." An icy rage sank through Janie as she shook her head. "That's the most lazy, self-consumed thing you can do."

"Would you rather have grown up with an alcoholic for a father?"

"I would have rather grown up with my *dad*. I would have rather you'd have taken responsibility and been the person you were supposed to have been. It's too late for that now—at least for me. But it's not for Livy."

Hunter stood and caught her hand. "Maybe we should go."

Yeah. They should. She'd told him this was a bad idea. But Hunter had said she needed to say the things she wanted. She had no idea she was going to take the course of champion for Olivia, but now that she'd started, she was going to finish.

Because it mattered. The ferocity of protectiveness crashed over her like an avalanche. *She had a little sister!* She was going to fight like a bear for her. Olivia was *not* going to grow up feeling like a cast-off, wondering what she did wrong. Not the way Janie had.

"Here's the thing. Livy will probably be okay. Now that I know she's my sister and that Bethany is okay with me being a part of her life, I'm going to do everything I can to make sure she knows that she is loved and has great value. But you?" Her voice cracked, lips trembled. "You will have missed it. You'll lose another daughter. You keep this course, and it'll happen all over again. And it will be your fault. Only yours. You want to live with that?"

Mike didn't meet her fiery gaze. He merely sat there slumped. Sulking. Hunter led her to the exit.

"One last thing." Janie turned from the door Hunter held open. "I was never lost. You knew exactly where I was the whole time. That's not going to change. Luna is always going to be my home. So if you want to reconcile ... if you truly want to have a relationship, you know where to find me."

CHAPTER
TWENTY-FOUR

"José had an update on his sister at study today."

Janie paused mid-scrub on one of her pie pans and looked over her shoulder at Hunter, who had been drying the dishes. "That sounds ominous."

"It's good news and bad news." He shelved the larger serving platter, then leaned against the bank of cabinets. "She's back home. Told her family she was sorry and the relationship was finished. Seems that something is still wrong though. Yesterday someone rear-ended her."

"Like an accident?"

Hunter shook his head, expression grave. "Hit-and-run. They don't have proof, but it seems like it was intentional."

Janie straightened and turned. "Why would they think that?"

"Isa noted the license plate number. The car that hit her is registered to the man's wife. The driver wasn't a woman, but it seems too much to be a coincidence."

"Oh my gosh." Janie's heart rate sped up at the thought of such a dangerous situation. "So it was like a warning or something?"

Hunter lifted one shoulder. "I don't know. But I told José what you and I have been praying about." He glanced at his feet. "I hope that's okay, Janie."

"Yeah." She crossed the floor until she stood in front of him, and touched his arm. "Yes. If she's in trouble, we should help. I can use her here, and I think Tara could use some help getting her clinic ready to open. Whatever it takes, we can make it work."

Hunter sighed, his body sagging. Clearly he was relieved as he slipped his arm around her and drew her against him. "Thank you." His lips pressed against her temple. "I know this isn't the easiest thing for you to do."

Janie snuggled in against him. "Keep a soft heart, right?"

He stroked the length of her hair. "Right. But if there's trouble, just talk to me. I'm on your side, okay?"

She leaned back and smirked at him. "I'm not a ridiculously jealous woman, Hunt."

A small grin lifted his lips. "No. But I'll be honest—I'm not completely upset that you *were* jealous of her."

"Hmm." She thunked his chest with two fingers. "Then I guess I'll have to admit that it was a *little* bit nice that you were jealous of Grady."

"Madly jealous, just so we're clear." He leaned down and kissed the end of her nose. "Let's never do that to each other again."

Janie slipped a hand around his neck and stared into those wonderfully familiar brown eyes. "I promise, Hunt. There's only space in my heart for one man, and you've claimed it."

"Hazel, it's good to see you up and going again." Mama B stepped beside Hazel on the boardwalk. "Bennett and Tara said that flu wanted to trounce you."

"I can't remember ever being that sick, that's for sure." She'd been on that sofa for five days, fevering then shivering. Coughing. Aching. It'd been downright awful. She couldn't imagine how badly Hunter must have felt when his illness had been so severe that he'd landed in a hospital.

All through it, Bennett, and then his mom, Tara, had been there with her. Making sure she stayed hydrated. Administering medication. Taking care of her animals. Keeping her cabin warm.

What might have happened to her back when she had no one?

Such things had never crossed her mind before. Miss independent and stubborn to a fault had never considered that she might need someone to be there for her at some point in time.

Seemed her carefully walled-up world of Hazel-lives-alone was crumbling more and more every day. First, she found herself trekking up to the Black Gulch, wondering why it was so important for her to rail against the peak that had overseen her parents' death. Then she felt compelled to read the words of a man who disrupted her slumbering soul with propositions like *If we find ourselves with a desire that nothing in this world can satisfy, the most probable explanation is that we were made for another world.*

And things only got stranger from there. How could she have the audacity—the insanity—to believe that she could *hear* the heavens sing?

But I did.

Could a broken heart make one lose their mind? She squeezed her eyes shut and there found her beloved, tenderly fingering her hair, pressing her burning face with his cool hand. *I am here now.* As he would always be . . . if she'd let him. Had that been his honest implication?

Goodness, she was a whirlwind of chaos and nonsense. And now this?

Opening her eyes, she looked up at the building at the end of the boardwalk. Tall and narrow, made of stone and timber. A pair of stained-glass windows flanking either side of the double front door. A cross hung above that entry.

"Will you be joining us today?"

Hazel started, turning a wide glance toward the woman. She'd forgotten MB stood beside her. Perhaps she was not yet well?

"I—" That was why she'd come, borrowing her brother's truck to drive that winding road to town.

Mama B wrapped an arm around her shoulder and squeezed. "There's always a spot for you beside me." Then she rubbed Hazel's back and continued down the walk, up the steps, and into that little stone building.

"What am I doing?" Hazel went over the morning that had led her here. She'd woken far more easily than she had in a week, feeling more herself. After a cup of tea and finishing her chores, she'd sat at her table.

And the loneliness had sunk in. Chilled and hollow and so vast she felt she might drown. The sensation was so awful, she thought she might prefer the flu. At least then Bennett had been there. And Tara.

She'd felt loved. Seen. Cared for.

Blowing out a breath of frustration, she had risen, refilled her tea, and retrieved the two books on her nightstand. Nana's copy of an anthology of Lewis's works and the Bible Bennett had gifted her.

She couldn't make sense of either.

She couldn't escape them either.

And then the church had entered her mind. A place she'd been to a few times. Bennett and Tara and MB would be there. It would stem the loneliness and possibly remind her why she didn't go there.

Music cut through the thin mountain air, replacing the silence with melody. *Did I really hear the stars sing?*

Her mind continued swirling, taking her heart along for the spin. What was wrong with her? Was she truly losing her mind.

Perhaps you are finding something.

What?

"What will I find?" she whispered. The question broke open a gush of many more. What would this cost? Would it be worth it? Would she ever be the same?

Hazel clenched her fists and turned away from the church as the answers feathered the fringes of her mind.

The cost? She would have to surrender everything. All of her independence, her insecurities. Her selfishness. And she would never be the same.

What would she find in return? And would it be worth it?

With all the chaos binding her heart and mind, she could not imagine the answer to either.

Even so, it beckoned.

***

Hunter took the ridge trail at a slow pace, praying as he walked through the mud. Hazel had come to church. On her own. Willingly.

Shock didn't go far enough to explain what he felt. Excitement. Yes, that too. And hope. But as he came to the bend that put Hazel's cabin in view, nerves twisted knots in his stomach. Who was he to speak of God to his sister. He was still a new Christian. There was so much he couldn't answer for her—like the question she'd flung at him up at the Black Gulch—*why had God let their parents die?* Likely, he would never know.

But he did know for sure what he had told her that day. God is real, and He cares. He breathed life into Hunter's lost soul, and He could do so for Hazel too. If he never understood any more about God than that, it was more than enough.

Hazel stepped out of her cabin, her pack of dogs tumbling outside behind her, as Hunter jogged down the last hill. She looked his way and waited until he made it to the steps to the deck.

"I wondered if you would come this way today."

"You came to church."

She nodded, her hand gripping the deck railing. "I figured you would either want to talk about that or the fact that I stole your truck to do so."

Hunter chuckled. It'd been good luck, as far as he was concerned, that he'd stayed with Mama B when he and Janie had returned Saturday night, which left his truck at the lodge. "You're welcome to take it whenever you need, Zel."

She flashed him a half grin. Then she stared out over the lake, the melting waters shimming in the sunshine, a contrast against the white ice that still remained in patches.

"Want to talk about it?" Hunter pressed, unsure that he should do so.

Shrugging, Hazel leaned back and then sighed. "I can't pretend God isn't real anymore. Everything around me tells me He's there." With a rare vulnerability open in her gaze, Hazel looked up at Hunter. "And lately, it's like He's . . . He's tracking me."

Hunter chuckled at her metaphor. "That's not a bad thing."

"I just don't know what to do with Him."

"Have you asked Him?"

"I wouldn't even know how to do that." Her gaze turned pleading. "So I guess I'm asking you. You didn't believe in God—or if you did, you didn't like Him. That's changed, and you've changed. Bennett changed, and he says it's because of faith. But I don't understand any of this. Lewis says something like God is what we need most and yet the thing we most fear. I feel this is true. I am scared of Him, yet I want to know Him. And I don't get it."

Already, there was such depth to the conversation. Hunter prayed he would not fail in this opportunity. *God, let your Spirit speak.* And then gripping her shoulder, he told her of the God who could not keep countenance with sin, but rather than losing forever all people who sinned, became a man who would die to pay for the penalty for that sin.

"God died?"

"Jesus died on the cross for us, Zel." Something they had learned about when they were kids going to church with MB and Janie. Somehow, it had never made sense until Hunter had known deeply that he needed saved. He prayed that now his sister would know it too and be saved. "He was God and King, and yet He was willing to take our punishment so that, even though we are rebellious and ugly to him and to others, we could be washed clean and declared right with Him."

Hazel's brow furrowed. She thought silently for several heartbeats and then pinned a skeptical look on Hunter. "This is why Lewis says we need God the most but are most terrified of Him too?"

Hunter nodded, surprised at her connection. He'd not made it on his own.

"Then how do you go from terrified to safe?"

"Do you have Nan's Bible?"

Hazel shook her head. "No, but I have one Bennett gave me."

Ah. Of course Bennett would have given her a Bible. "Can you get it for me?"

With a nod, Hazel went inside and, after a brief moment, came back out.

Hunter took the book she held out to him, shuffled through the fine pages until he came to Acts 16:31. The passage that John had shown him when Hunter had first come to believe. "Here." He pointed. "Read this."

Hazel leaned over his arm. "'Believe on the Lord Jesus Christ and you will be saved.'" She looked up at him. "That's it? Believe in Jesus?"

Hunter nodded, then turned the pages again until he came to Romans 10. "Here now, read verses nine and ten."

Again, she leaned in. "'If you declare with your mouth, "Jesus is Lord," and believe in your heart that God raised him from the dead, you will be saved. For it is with your heart that you believe and are justified, and it is with your mouth that you profess your faith and are saved.'" And again she looked up at Hunter, traces of confusion on her face. "Saved . . . from the terror?"

He nodded. "The terror comes from knowing, deep inside, that we are separated from God. Because we sin—we rebel against Him. Do things we shouldn't to ourselves and to others. Deny Him and refuse to love Him as He should be loved." Did he get that right? It was how he understood sin.

Please, Lord, help me to say right things . . .

"How . . . how is this done?" Hazel asked.

A recent memory of something Hunter had read flashed through his mind. "John and I have been reading through some of the life and prayers of Martin Luther. He was a great Christian—a man who yearned for a God he could love when all he knew was a God he was terrified of."

"And?" Hazel bent forward with near desperation.

"He threw his heart to Christ and said, 'I am yours. Save me.'"

For a long moment Hazel stared at him. Was there wonder in those brown-green eyes? Then her lids slipped shut, and she whispered, "I am yours. Save me." Her brows knitted and blinked at Hunter. "He will save me? Bring me from fear into love?"

"He died to save you, Hazel. If He did that and rose again from the grave, there's no reason to think that He wouldn't do what He says. Cast your heart on Him and believe. That is what He asks."

CHAPTER
TWENTY-FIVE

ISA SEEMED NO WORSE for the wear.

Janie puzzled over the young woman's determined perkiness. She'd moved into one of Mama's spare rooms over the weekend and had worked two days at the café. There'd been no trace of remorse in Isa's mannerisms. She smiled brightly, laughed merrily—if not boisterously. And most puzzling, flirted almost nonstop.

It was a consolation of sorts to see that the girl did so with every male who came through Janie's door.

Was this truly a simple factor of Isa's personality? Sort of like Gemma, and even Janie herself, who leaned into over-positivity when they were stressed? Perhaps. Seemed like maybe this determined flirtation went beyond covering up distress though. Like it went all the way to outright rebellion—the kind that dug its heels in and declared herself unbeatable.

Which perhaps meant that beneath those sassy grins and winking brown eyes, there was a young woman thrashing against something awful. Something that *was* beating her.

Lord, give me wisdom. And keep my heart soft.

Janie whispered the prayer under her breath as she pushed through the swinging door into the café's dining room.

"I believe I can convert you to a coffee man." Isa pocketed her notepad, placed a hand on her hip, and let that sassy grin light up her pretty face. "You just need the right barista. I'm your girl."

Sixteen-year-old Mack Ritten looked up at her like a smitten puppy. Then he let a lopsided grin tease his lips. "I might take that bet. What do I get when I win?"

Isa smirked, tilting her chin to the side. "Now, Mack. We are just talking about a *friendly* bet here. Don't go getting ideas . . ."

"Oh, I have ideas."

Straightening, Isa never let her smile slip. "Me too. I think a caramel macchiato will do the trick. Then you can run on back to school and let you're classmates know your grown up enough to drink coffee." She spun away from the table, likely after dropping a quick wink, and sauntered back to the counter.

Janie sighed. She slid the larger platter of spiced pear turnovers into the pastry case and then met Isa at the coffee machine.

"Ease up a bit, hmm?"

A pair of wide, innocent brown eyes met Janie's mild reprimand. "What does that mean?"

"You're flirting."

"What?"

"That kid is barely old enough to drive."

Isa tossed her hair and shrugged. "Oh, it doesn't mean anything. He knows that."

"Isa." Janie waited until the young woman looked at her. "I mean it. Ease up on the flirting. Friendliness is great. Flirting . . . not so much. It could get you into trouble."

Isa's bright expression darkened into a full scowl. "What is that supposed to mean?"

Frustrated, and with a sharp stab of guilt, Janie sighed. "It means what I said. I want this to work out for you. For both of us. But you have to pull back on the flirting."

For a moment Isa continued to frown. Then, as if shooing a fly away, she brushed off the conversation, tipped up her chin, and nodded. "You got it, Boss." And . . . there was that smile. Not really flirty, because it was aimed at Janie and not someone of the male variety. But certainly cheeky.

Certain she hadn't gotten through, Janie rolled her eyes and turned back to the counter. There, watching that exchange, sat Grady. Her stomach tightened, particularly at the man's frown. Grady was a pleasant man. Easygoing. Friendly. She'd never seen him sour.

Then again, she had ditched him back in Arizona.

Then again, again, he'd told her to.

Boy, this morning was going all topsy-turvy.

Putting on her big-girl panties, so to speak, Janie crossed the space between them. "Grady, it's good to see you."

His smile surfaced readily enough. Relief plunged through her.

"How long have you been back?"

He leaned his arms against the blue-stained pine. "I've been back and forth for a while now. Wasn't sure . . ."

Janie leaned a hip against the counter. "You're always welcome here."

He nodded. "I hoped so."

Her heart pinched at his reserve. She'd really messed that up. Didn't he know it was her fault? Or was he embarrassed about the whole thing? Once again that was her fault too. She was the one to be embarrassed, not him.

"What can I get you?" She pushed off the counter and pointed to the pastry cabinet. "I just pulled those spiced pear turnovers out of the oven."

"Sounds perfect."

"And coffee?"

"You bet." Grady's attention wandered to Isa, who was wiping down the table where Mack had been sitting. "Looks like you've taken on new help."

"Yeah. Just a couple of days ago."

"She's gonna be handful." He planted a knowing look on Janie. "That's Isa, right?"

"Yeah." So he remembered seeing her that day at the lodge. Not that Janie thought he'd forget.

"Seems . . . awkward."

Janie plated a turnover and filled a clean mug with black coffee. She set both in front of him. "Maybe a little."

"I got the impression she wasn't from Luna."

"She's not. But she's trying it on for size."

One dark eyebrow arched against Grady's forehead. Janie shrugged, knowing there was a question there but also knowing she shouldn't divulge too much of the story. Isa could make her own impressions, good or bad. Didn't need rumors flying around town to do it for her. Not that Grady was a gossip.

"Truth is, with me and Hunter getting married soon and the lodge opening, I needed to find some help." Janie took a breath and gauged Grady's reaction. His steady expression didn't hint at anything more than a man listening to a story. "Isa wanted to try a different scene, so we thought this might work out."

Grady nodded. Slowly.

"Look." Janie leaned forward, planting her elbows on the counter and lowering her voice. "What happened up at the bonfire was my fault. Mine and Hunter's. Isa didn't know anything about it—not any more than you did."

A touch of pink crept into his face. "I knew . . ."

She pulled back. "What?"

He rubbed the back of his neck. "I mean, I didn't know all the details. But I could tell that you and Hunter had history. That was kind of hard to miss."

Janie stared at the counter, not sure what to say. "I'm sorry, Grady."

"We've been over that." He slid a hand nearer and tapped the counter next to her hand. "There are no hard feelings over here."

Janie lifted her eyes to meet his, finding kind sincerity staring back at her. "So we're friends."

"Absolutely."

That made her day better.

Nerves spiraled through Bennett's gut, quite possibly worse than if he were about to line up to the starting line himself. Man, he wanted Nathan to do well—to feel good about all the genuine hard work he'd been putting in. And to enjoy this quirky activity he'd found.

Standing alongside the colorful flag tape that marked the race boundary at the start, Bennett watched while Hazel went over final checks with Nathan. His .22 must have checked clear, because he secured the over-the-shoulder sling and cinched it down tight against his back. Then he checked the ammo pouch at his hip. A count, a nod from Hazel. Must be good.

Hazel gave him a few more instructions, and as she was talking, a girl in green race pants and a white gilet skied toward them. She sidestepped until she was next to Nathan and smiled up at him, her brown braids poking out of her white-and-green headband.

Nathan matched the girl's grin, then gestured to Hazel. With a pleasant expression, the pretty little thing reached a gloved hand forward and shook Hazel's hand.

Ella Hammond. Had to be the girl Hunter had mentioned when this whole biathlon thing had first come up.

As he watched the interaction, Bennett had to admit the little thing on skis didn't look anything like he'd imagined. Particularly when it came to the type of girl who would catch Nathan's eye. He'd pictured a scowling teenager with dyed black hair and a lip ring. Someone who flashed trouble on her expression as clearly as the snow shone in the bright winter sun.

This girl in the braids looked about as sweet and charming as they came.

"I haven't missed anything important, have I?"

Bennett's mind hit a hard stop and his shoulders rammed straight. He turned, found Chip—*Dad!*—rubbing his hands together. All Bennett could do was gawk.

"Surprise!" Chip grinned as if he were Santa Claus.

"Dad." Bennett fought the urge to step back. "You're here."

"You bet. When Nathan told me about the race today—and that it would be his first—I decided I couldn't miss it."

Bennett blinked. Nathan had only just spoken to their father three days ago. It had been the standard weekly phone call. "How long have you been back in the country?"

"Oh." Chip looked away. Then his *everything is great* charade fell back onto his expression, and he waved off the question. "Not long. Perfect timing, right?"

Liar.

Chip Crofton was a habitual liar. And something warned Bennett that he hadn't shown up in Montana with the sole intention of watching his son's first biathlon. If that sort of thing had mattered that much to the man, he'd have come to see the kids at Christmas. As it was, he'd barely eked out a phone call on that holiday.

"Racers, find your start."

Bennett focused on the gathering of thirty-plus skiers at the line and picked out Nathan. He posed at the ready, little Ella on his right.

Hazel slipped beside Bennett, drawing a quick glance from him. She smiled up, her joy wonderfully obvious in those dancing brown eyes. For a moment he wished he could tuck her close to his side. Or at least take her hand and squeeze it.

Friends didn't do things like that though. Did they?

"Is this your mountain princess?" The question came from his left.

Bennett ignored it while the starter raised his gun. "Take your mark."

The crowd stilled, as if every person held their breath.

"Set."

Fire stirred in Bennett's belly. *Please, Lord, let Nathan have fun and do well.*

The report of a shot rang through the clean mountain air. The field of competitors took off, the tails of their skis kicking up powder as they pushed forward toward the first decline, where they'd gain speed.

"Go Nathan!" Hazel jumped and clapped.

Bennett grinned and joined her cheering. "Go get it, buddy!" He looked down at Hazel the same moment she looked up at him. Her cheeks flushed with enthusiasm and mountain chill and the joy dancing in her eyes . . .

He did exactly what he said he shouldn't, pulling her close and even leaning his face into her hair. She smelled of blueberries and vanilla, and as she pressed into his side, the line of friendship they'd drawn became blurry.

They were good together. Couldn't she see that? Didn't she want what they had shared back—and to last forever?

"You must be Bennett's mountain princess." Chip shoved his way in front of them, taking Hazel by the arm. Without considering that she may not be comfortable with it, he pulled her in for a full hug.

Bennett didn't miss the way her spine jammed straight.

"Dad." Taking Hazel's elbow, he gently tugged her back.

"What? I can't hug your girlfriend?"

Hazel looked toward their boots, adjusting her stocking cap.

Man, this was so uncomfortable. "Maybe you should try getting her name first. And asking if she's okay with a hug."

"Aw, Bennett." Chip waved him off. "You're being stiff. Lighten up."

"I'm going to go to the first checkpoint." Hazel's eyes grazed over Bennett's face, and then she took off at a jog.

"What's a checkpoint?" Chip asked.

"A spot where you can see the course. I think it's at the 1k mark."

"Will we see them pass by here again?"

"Yes. The shooting range is just over this hill, and they'll finish at the start."

"Perfect. We can wait here then."

"I'd planned to go with Hazel."

"Hazel. That's her name. Surely she doesn't mind *mountain princess* though."

"I wouldn't bet on it." Not from Chip. And not given that currently she wasn't Bennett's anything other than friend.

But Dad was going to do what he wanted. Just like he always did.

"Listen, you can stay here. I'm going—"

"Hold up, son."

Bennett cringed. *Son* was not a term of endearment when it came to Chip. It was a lead in to some kind of manipulation.

"What?"

"I need to talk to you."

"It can wait. Nathan has been working really hard on this, and I don't want to miss it. You shouldn't either. After all, you said you came all this way to watch him." Bennett waited for his dad to take that bait.

With a mild scowl, Chip nodded and gestured forward, as if to say *lead the way.* Bennett did, and from that moment until the end of the race, they were too busy traversing the course to have time to talk. Thank goodness.

Nathan did well, considering it was his first time. Seventh overall, fourth in his division.

"If I did better on that second round of shooting, I maybe would have placed second." He was all excitement as he discussed the race with Hazel. "That one cost me three penalty laps. But the skiing felt good."

"We'll keep working on it." Hazel patted his shoulder. "And your skiing was impressive."

"Nice job, Ella," Nathan said.

The girl in the green and white stopped and smiled. Those brown braids looked like they'd not been disturbed the whole race, even though she'd flown through the course all three laps.

"You won, right?" Bennett asked.

"Yes." She ducked shyly. "But that's not nearly as impressive as Nate. I've been doing this for years, but this was his first race, and he made top ten. That's amazing."

"Thanks." Nathan blushed. Blushed! And *Nate?*

Bennett buckled in a grin.

"I'll see you at school." Ella raised a hand as she moved across the field of visiting competitors and spectators.

"Yeah. See ya."

Hazel and Bennett exchanged glances. Chip strode right into Nathan's space, laughing loudly. "She's a cute one, Nate."

Nathan's glow immediately dimmed. He stiffened, shrugged off Dad's arm, and scowled. "It's Nathan, Dad. And what are you doing here?"

"Wow. How's that for a welcome?" Chip shook his head but kept grinning, like this was all a game. "I come halfway across the country to see you ski, and that's all you've got?"

While everyone around continued to chat and laugh, the little group around Nathan became wooden and silent. Nathan looked at Bennett, as if to ask for help.

"Thanks for coming, Dad." Bennett nearly choked out the sentence.

"Yeah," Nathan mumbled. "Thanks."

"What's a father for?" Chip said.

A whole lot more than what Chip seemed capable of.

Bennett moved around their dad. "If you clip out of your skis, I'll take them to the car."

Nathan nodded, misery darkening his eyes.

This was not how his first race should have gone. Not at all.

CHAPTER
TWENTY-SIX

HAZEL FOUND BENNETT ALONE in a corner booth at Janie's Café, mug of coffee basically untouched. She'd known that he'd spent the afternoon with his dad, so it didn't surprise her to have spied him walking alone ten minutes earlier. When it came to his dad, Bennett had a limited amount of tolerance.

She slipped into the opposite bench, glad to have the opportunity to talk. She had something really important to tell him. But his glance at her barely produced the smallest of smiles. He looked . . . devastated.

"Bennett, what's wrong?" Hazel whispered.

He visibly swallowed, then shook his head. "Long day. *Really* long day." He looked down at the mug, and Hazel had a strong suspicion he wished there was something stronger than coffee in it.

Uncertainty wove through her. Maybe this wasn't the time to tell him about her conversation with Hunter. About her newfound faith. Instead, she focused on the good things they'd shared earlier that day.

"Nathan did really well today."

Bennett nodded and attempted another smile. This one was marginally more successful. "Yeah, he did. Thanks to you."

A brush of heat touched her cheeks. "I am enjoying it. It's nice to have a reason to hang out." Would he understand her subtlety?

His hand slipped off the mug and slid toward hers, stopping just short of it. When the craving for his touch nearly overwhelmed her, the tip of his fingers skimmed her knuckles.

Oh, how she missed him.

His stare settled on her, and she found herself swimming in that blue gaze, a mixture of longing and delight filling her heart.

"I wanted to tell you something," she whispered.

She nearly missed his slight nod but felt keenly the deepening intensity in his eyes.

"I . . . I believe." Is that how one said it? Hazel wasn't sure she had the right words. Was there a formal declaration she was supposed to know? To say?

Bennett blinked and leaned closer. "You believe?"

Hazel's lips trembled. She was getting this wrong. *God, I'm new at this . . . please help!* She nodded. "I asked Jesus to save me."

Suddenly tears swam in those beautiful blue eyes. "Hazel," he breathed. Then he clamped a hand on hers, pulled it to his lips, and pressed a kiss to her knuckles. "That is the best news."

His reaction overwhelmed her—as if this mattered to him more than all the world.

"Thank you for telling me." He kept a firm hold on her hand. "I needed some good news today."

Her heart fell from hope and delight to worry. "What happened today?"

His jaw clenched hard, and that sheen in his eyes returned. After a clear fight for control, Bennett let loose a quivering breath. "My dad . . . he says the kids are to go home."

"Home?" Panic struck her heart. "You mean back to Chicago?"

He nodded, a tear flicking from one eye.

No!

Hazel rose from her seat and turned to slide in next to him. Without hesitation he hauled her in his arms. Beneath her hands, his chest quavered.

"When?" she whispered.

"He says now. They are to go back with him when he leaves."

She shook her head.

"I won't let that happen. Even if I have to take him to court." Hard determination chiseled his voice. "They should be able to finish out the school year here."

Hazel leaned back. "What can I do?"

Misery writhed his handsome face. "You believe?"

She nodded.

"Then pray, Hazel. For me and for the kids. And for my dad."

"Your dad?"

He nodded, though he ducked. "Yes. Him most of all."

Janie hunched over her notebook, checking off items on her to-do list. It'd been nice having Isa around to do the cleanup and carry the slow hours. It had given Janie time to plan and make sure everything was done.

She scanned the check marks and compared them to the items still yet to do. The number done now out-marked the number left open. She grinned.

It was all coming together. And in just a week, it would be all done.

With all her heart, Janie looked forward to that. Not that she hadn't enjoyed wedding planning—it'd been fun. The decorations were lovely, and they would serve the lodge well for years to come. Her dress was simple but elegant, and she enjoyed a thrill as she imagined Hunter's eyes lighting up when he first caught a glimpse of her in it. The cake would be delicious.

But none of that truly mattered a whole lot. Not when she compared it to the life she and Hunter would make together. *That* was the part she was most excited about.

With joy bubbling up in her middle, Janie picked up her notebook and pen and started for the kitchen door. "I'm just going to run upstairs and make a phone call about the cake," she said to Isa as she went.

Isa glanced up from the mugs she was putting away and nodded. "I've got it, Boss." Even as she spoke, the bell above the café door chimed, and Isa turned to welcome their customer with a cheerful "Hi there!"

Hunter had been right. Isa was a good worker for Janie, though she did still flirt a whole awful lot. So far that hadn't caused any trouble. And it did bring in a few more high school boys after school. Even though she was in her early twenties, maybe Isa needed a little more time to grow up a bit.

Heaven knew Janie hadn't been the smartest or most mature at that age.

She took the steps two at a time, burst through her apartment, and quickly made her phone call. All was on schedule, and the cake would be delivered to the lodge the morning of the wedding. Using her fine-point Sharpie, Janie added another check mark.

Sure that Isa had the dining room handled, Janie freshened up her makeup. No more than ten minutes passed and she was back downstairs and nearly through the door.

"Look, I'm not sure what I've done to upset you, but I'd sure like to know why you're so sour at me."

Janie froze. She'd never heard that tone from Isa. Serious, cold, and a little . . . hurt? Had a customer been rude to her? There were a few in town who could be snippy. But Isa had already encountered those people, and she'd handled them with sugar.

What was going on?

"I think you can pour a cup of coffee without all the added attention."

Was that . . .

"Added attention? What does that mean?"

"It means I don't have time for a reckless flirt."

Janie peeked through the small window on the door and sucked in a sharp breath. There he was. Crisp button-down tucked into his uniform pants. Game and Parks hat pulled low on his brow. And a deep frown marring his otherwise pleasant face.

Grady. Grady Briggs wore the deepest scowl possible and kept it pinned right on Isa.

What on earth had happened?

CHAPTER
TWENTY-SEVEN

JANIE BREATHED IN DEEPLY as she and Hunter strolled off the deck
and toward the edge of Elk Pond. A sweet taste of new life filled
the cool air as the setting sun stained the evening sky in pastel pinks
and apricot. The rippling water, most of which was free of ice, was
a richly hued watercolor reflection of dark peaks and warm colors.

The perfect end to the eve of their wedding.

Vehicles backed out and drove away, their tires a sloshy crunch against the freshly graveled drive, as the gathering left the rehearsal dinner. It'd all gone so well—their wedding practice and the meal to follow. All that stood between her and Hunter now was less than twenty-four hours.

"Hurry up, sun."

Hunter chuckled, squeezing her hand. At the edge of the water, he turned. "I agree." He tipped his face in the direction of the waning light. "Hurry up so I can marry this woman already." Then he looked back at her, grasping her other hand so he held them both.

"Will you be going out to make the most of you last night as a free man?" Janie asked.

"No." He leaned down until his forehead rested against hers. "I'm not losing freedom. I'm gaining a wife. The girl I've been in love with since I was a kid. So I'll be going to bed, praying I sleep hard so the night isn't long. And then I'll wake up ready to promise you forever."

"Hmm." Janie grinned as she brushed her nose against his.

A long moment passed, the sound of a spring breeze moving the water and the soft beat of their hearts filling the gentle quiet.

"Janie?" His whisper spread warmth across her brow. "Will you think it silly if I pray right now?"

Her heart oozed warmth as she moved her hands to his chest. "Silly? No. I would love it."

"I'm still not very good at it."

"Is there a meter stick you use to measure?"

He shook his head, but his intense gaze remained serious. "I want so much to be a godly man, but I feel so . . . behind. I see John and watch José, the sort of husbands that they are—the sort of men they are—and I feel inspired and yet terribly inadequate at the same time."

Janie felt the prick of a tear at his honest vulnerability. "We'll learn and grow together, right?"

His sigh seemed to originate from his soul. "I just don't want to fail. Especially now that it's me and you."

She pressed on her toes to brush her lips against his. "Pray then, Hunter. Pray for us both."

Hunter cupped her shoulders in his hands and bowed his head. "God . . ." His voice trembled as he exhaled. "Father, I can't begin to say all that is welling in my heart right now. Thank You for this woman, for her love, and for the future we're stepping into. Show me how to be the husband she needs—the husband You want me to be. I feel . . . inadequate. Scared that I'll let her down. Probably I will, but when that happens, give me the humility to admit it, and give Janie the grace to forgive. Neither of us saw a good marriage growing up, so we don't really know how to do it. But we ask that You would show us. Teach us day by day how to love well. And make our home one that brings You glory."

As the light seeped away, leaving them in a tender darkness, Hunter wrapped his arms around Janie and pulled her close. She felt the shuddering of his breath before he whispered, "Amen."

The tears would not be held back. Janie tucked her face against his chest and slipped her arms around him. "Amen," she echoed.

Love. Gratitude. Joy. Her heart had never felt so full. God had worked something beautiful, that was for sure, and as glorious as the lake and the lodge were, they were nothing compared to this moment.

And it was only the beginning.

He couldn't believe he'd forgotten to bring his suit.

Bennett shook his head and grumbled *ridiculous* as he took the final curve into town from the lodge. Of all days to not be prepared, this was the one he chose to do something dumb. If only he'd realized somewhere during the morning, or even midafternoon, while they were setting up last-minute wedding details, that he'd not grabbed the garment bag in his closet!

With a quick flick of his wrist, he checked the time on his Garmin. Thirty-eight minutes until showtime. Man! That was cutting things way too close. He did not want to miss Hunter and Janie's wedding. Particularly, he didn't want to miss seeing Hazel in a dress—the one Janie somehow managed to beg her into wearing, as her only bridal attendant.

Even as he sped to his house, breaking to a stop with a hard jerk, Bennett grinned. Hazel . . . she was a beautiful woman in her flannels and jeans and boots. He had no doubt she'd be stunning in the ice-blue gown she was to wear this evening. And he certainly didn't want to miss the opportunity of telling her.

He had so many things he wanted to say to that woman.

With a fire fueling his go, Bennett raced into the house, shedding his sweatshirt as he ran to his room. Within five minutes, and a fury of clothes flying this way and that, leaving a mess, he had his suit in place. A quick check of the mirror and a touch up of his freshly clipped hair, he was off again. It was a twenty-minute drive back to the lodge. Fifteen if he pushed those narrow curves just past the point of comfort. He should have ten minutes to spare. He'd make it.

As he turned onto Main, which would lead him toward the trail back to the lodge, a flash of movement caught his eye within Janie's Café. Hadn't she closed it for the day?

She had. He was certain. But the lights were on, and through the windows, he spied a woman sweeping.

Isa?

She'd been invited to the wedding, hadn't she? No way Janie had excluded her. Especially when José and Rosalina were there—he'd seen them park as he was pulling out of the drive.

With another hard push on the brakes, Bennett stopped in the middle of the road, let himself out of the vehicle, and jogged to the café, only to find the front door locked.

Yeah, it was closed.

He tapped the window, drawing Isa's surprised attention. The girl frowned and wouldn't make eye contact as she unlocked the door and let him in.

"We're closed today."

"I know." Bennett came just inside. "There's a wedding. Pretty much the whole town is there."

"Yeah." Isa reached for the broom she'd propped on a table.

"Isa." He waited for her to look at him. "You were invited."

She shrugged.

"Is there a reason you're not there?"

Another shrug. "I thought I'd get some things done here."

"I think Janie would rather her one employee—and her new friend—would attend her wedding."

A slow, shuddered exhale audibly left Isa's lips. "I think it's better if I stay here."

What was going on? As far as he knew, things between Isa and Hunter and Janie were fine. The scene at the groundbreaking party had been forgotten. No, more than that—both Hunter and Janie had declared the entire fiasco their own fault and held neither Grady nor Isa responsible. Proof of all being well—Grady was up at the wedding this very moment. Bennett had seen him.

Something was wrong. But Bennett had no idea how to get to it, nor did he have the time to try. "Look, Isa. You're a part of this community now, and I know for a fact that Hunter and Janie are glad for it. Don't miss this opportunity to embrace that."

With a strained brow, Isa bit her lip. "I . . ."

"Go change. We have less than five minutes to get out of town if we're going to get there on time."

She held a hesitant look on him.

"Scoot!" He reached for the broom and shooed her toward the back door.

Isa nodded and ran for the door. As he waited, Bennett puzzled over her odd behavior. Isa was all energy and smiles and confidence—too much, oftentimes. This unsure withdrawal from her was concerning. Given that she'd moved to Luna because of a mess she'd gotten herself into, Bennett's concern ratcheted up.

He'd work on the truth later though. Right now, there was another issue he needed to think through.

Hazel.

She'd be at the front of the crowd, up there beside Janie. And he had no doubt she'd see Bennett there with Isa. He couldn't think of anything other than this not ending well.

Lifting his phone, he typed a hurried text. *Giving Isa a ride to the wedding. I'll explain later. Please don't jump to conclusions.* Send. Delivered.

And that was how that text stayed. Delivered. Most likely because Hazel didn't have her phone with her. She often left it at her cabin, and today she wouldn't feel any reason to try to figure out how to carry it while wearing a dress.

He typed out another hurried explanation and sent that text to Nathan, glad for at least the hundredth time that Chip had relented and allowed the kids to remain in Luna until the end of the school year. It was doubtful that Nathan would be able to relay the information to Hazel, but he could at least tell Gemma, and they could avoid whatever scene his sister might otherwise make.

Bennett sighed and lifted a prayer for help as he tucked his phone into the pocket inside his suit coat.

With one minute to spare before they would absolutely be late, Isa flew through the swinging door from the kitchen, wearing a simple olive-colored dress and a cream cardigan sweater. Her shoes dangled in one hand and a hair clip in the other.

"Ready?" he asked.

"Yes." She didn't stop to answer but burst through the front door. "I don't want you to be late because of me."

The drive up to the lodge might have been a good time to pull out of Isa why she'd suddenly decided to stay in Luna when everyone in town was up at the lodge. But Bennett was too preoccupied with the pending disaster he felt certain waited for him at the end of the day.

Yeah, he and Hazel were still in the friend zone. But that wasn't how he wanted things to stay. And while Hazel had become so much softer over the past months, he wouldn't blame her for making assumptions when he walked into the wedding with Isa. If things were reversed, he had to admit he'd be hurt and upset too.

If only Hazel had her phone with her.

Isa fixed her hair, twisting it up into some kind of messy elegance, and strapped her shoes on. Bennett found a spot along the drive and parked, but they'd have a jaunt to get to the lodge, with so many cars lined up ahead. He and Isa wasted no time leaving the Bronco, and he offered his arm to her for steadiness as they ran down the dirt drive.

Music floated from the lodge in front of them—the type that indicated the ceremony was starting.

"I'm sorry," Isa said.

"We'll get in." And hopefully not make a scene.

When they made it to the open front doors, it was in time to see Hazel finish her walk down the beautifully decorated stairway. Nathan, acting as an usher in Bennett's place, saw Bennett and Isa and strode to meet them. He looked grown up and quite good, his hair tied back in a man bun and his new suit tailored just right. With a subtle nod, he indicated a pair of open seats near the back on the bride's side, right next to Grady Briggs.

The gathering stood to their feet as the bridal-entry song began. With a nod of thanks to Nathan, Bennett took Isa's arm, and they scurried to the open spots before Janie began her way down the stairs. Isa stopped short when Bennett gestured for her to take the seat beside Grady. But then she ducked her head and filled the spot. Bennett stepped in beside her and looked up to see the bride begin her descent.

Janie looked lovely, her cream gown a simple V-neck that fit her perfectly, and a spray of flowers in her dark hair rather than a veil. Bennett turned to witness Hunter's reaction at seeing his bride. Pure, radiant, thrilling love lit his friend's face. At his side, Hunter's best man, John Brighton, gripped Hunter's shoulder, as if to hold him steady, knowing the electrifying jolt that had just slammed through the groom.

Bennett chuckled. Then he met Hazel's watch, pinned on him. She looked away the moment he made eye contact. But not before he saw her wince.

His chest clenched hard as he felt keenly Isa's presence at his side. Hazel had definitely misunderstood.

"Hazel, it can't be what it looks like." Janie squeezed Hazel's hand as they stood in the receiving line, leaning in close to whisper. "There has to be some kind of explanation."

Hazel looked at her friend, grateful for her steady love. Such a kindness, that Janie would worry about her when this was Janie's wedding day. Hazel shook her head. "The most reasonable explanation is the obvious one. Bennett has moved on."

Janie clenched her jaw. "I don't believe that." But as she glanced down the way toward the gathering of people, straight at Bennett and Isa, doubt filtered through her expression.

"Don't worry, Janie."

Janie pinned her attention back on Hazel.

Hazel gave her a wobbly smile. "I won't cause a scene."

"I wasn't worried about that."

Hazel gave her a wry grin. "Yes you were."

A pathetic laugh crossed Janie's mouth. "I wouldn't blame you."

A twist of nausea rolled through Hazel's tummy as she looked at the handsome man she'd always love. It was as she'd fearfully predicted. She had lost him. But she had no one to blame but herself.

"He deserves happiness," Hazel said. "And goodness knows I had my chance. Anyway, this is your wedding day. Long overdue. Worry is not allowed."

"Zel—" The line moved forward before Janie could finish, bringing a rush of well-wishers toward them.

The rest would be left unsaid. Likely for the best.

Hazel sent a silent prayer, the newness of the act bittersweet in that moment. *Please help me to be good.* And then she braced herself against the ache as the man she loved came nearer, another woman at his side.

A long breath. Another painful stab through her heart. And a forced smile. She would make it through, and she would be kind. For Janie's sake. And for Bennett's.

Because love wasn't selfish.

CHAPTER
TWENTY-EIGHT

HUSBAND AND WIFE. HAZEL mulled over that phrase, applying it to her brother and her best friend. It no longer felt like a foreign threat—a risk too great to take. For Hunter and Janie, it felt like a beautiful magic. Like the unfurling of a columbine plant from the chilly, thawed spring earth.

New life. Beautiful hope. Promise.

Standing on the dock, still dressed in the bridesmaid gown that wasn't nearly as awful as she'd feared it would be, Hazel tightened the blanket she'd plucked from her couch around her shoulders. It was the blue one—the one Bennett had tucked around her when she'd had the flu.

New life. Beautiful hope. Promise.

How could her heart move with such an aching joy? How could there exist, in the same moment, the pain of surrendering to a loss—the one that was her and Bennett—and a sweet steadiness of hope in spite of heartache?

She lifted her gaze from the lapping waters of the lake, whose surface reflected the gentle light of the full moon, to the vast kingdom of stars that emerged, yet again to sing praise to their Maker.

"Lord, how your wonders are displayed, where'er we turn our eyes, if we survey the ground we tread or gaze upon the skies." She spoke the second part of the second verse of Isaac Watts's hymn. Clenching the blanket to her chest, a sudden burst of deep emotion ruptured in her heart. She shuddered at its strength, and from her mouth came a trembling laugh/cry. "Or look upon this heart, awakened by Your love. Your wonder given to this selfish, lost soul."

Magic. Miracle. Whatever the name one gave it. It was the power of God to transform a life. Even a hard, selfish, cold life such as hers.

"Do you hear the anthem of the cosmos this evening?"

Hazel startled at Bennett's soft voice and turned to see the man step onto the dock. In the light of the moon, his dark suit looked sleek, and his freshly shaven face and newly cut hair made him appear as he had when they'd first clashed—dangerously handsome.

But he wasn't dangerous. He was good. So good. The kind of goodness that comes from a man whose heart is surrendered to the Love of all loves.

A fresh quiver shook her chest. She'd never stop loving this man, even if he did move on and find the happiness he deserved with someone else. With Isa.

There was that ache. Sharp enough to catch her breath.

Bennett stopped his stride two steps from her. "Can you hear it again?"

She placed her attention back upon the sky. "Not like that one night." There was a sad sort of yielding in that. "I think that was a solitary event."

"Perhaps. Until this life peels back and we see the fullness of God's kingdom. Then . . ." He chuckled, rocking back on his heels. "Then I think we'll be stunned at all that is glorious and discover that even with all that is wonderous around us, we only saw a glimpse."

"Hmm." She smiled even as tears burned her eyes. "It's enough though, isn't it?"

"Enough to know that God is?"

"Yes. And that He loves."

The touch of his hand against hers made her twitch, and after a quick suck of air, she gently pulled her fingers away. She didn't want to be a petty woman. Not the ugly, impulsive selfish girl she'd been most of her life. But didn't he know she couldn't handle this?

Didn't he know her heart was breaking?

"Zel."

Her jaw trembled at the sound of her name on his breath, spoken with a quiet tenderness that made her head swim.

She reached past the pleasant fuzziness and into the reality of the evening. Finding it, she ironed her posture. "Isa looked happy to be a part of things today."

Bennett turned to face her. "I didn't bring her as a date, and she understood that."

Hazel swallowed. From her observation of the pair of them that evening, that was true. They didn't act like . . . like a couple. But it still stung.

"Hazel." Bennett reached to grip her shoulders with both hands. "I gave her a ride so she wouldn't be left out. There was nothing more to it than that."

She nodded.

"Even so, I know how it must have looked to you."

She bit her bottom lip. "It's not really my business either way."

"You were kind. Gracious."

Emotion rippled through her, causing her body to shake.

"Thank you." Bennett rubbed her arms. "I know it probably wasn't easy, and I'm proud of the way you handled yourself."

Daring to peek at him, Hazel couldn't stop the truth from tumbling across her lips. "I was dying inside, Bennett. Thinking that you've moved on."

He held her gaze for what felt like the life of her heart, and then he shook his head. Those warm, gentle hands moved from her arms to cup her jaw, and he lowered his head.

Slowly. So achingly slow. His warm breath, tinged with sweet white wine, fanned over her lips.

Her yearning for his kiss flared to near desperation.

"That's never going to happen." Though spoken in a low, quiet tone, his words held the severity of an oath. "I'm never getting over you, Zel. I'm never even going to try."

The wanting was too much. She closed the wisp of air between her mouth and his, releasing her grip on the blanket, and it fell to the planks as she gripped the lapel of his suit coat. His kiss was slow and deep. One full of long-kept desire and unmovable promise.

The love of this man . . .

She didn't deserve it. Hadn't understood it. And mysteriously, was unable to quench it.

Faithful. That was what Bennett Crofton had become. To his God, his beliefs, and—stunningly—to her.

She pulled back from the joy of his kisses as the full impact of wonder set in. "You love me," she whispered.

"I do."

"No matter what."

"Yes."

A cry ripped through her heart. One of remorse, but also of cleansing. How shallow she had seen love. Like imagining a little handful of rain splatter gathered in the pit of a stone, when really it was the ocean.

But the deep had burst forth in her soul. No more fear. No more selfishness.

She curled her fingers into the soft thickness of his hair and stared into those beautiful eyes. "I love you, Bennett Crofton."

His lids slid shut, and he pressed his forehead to hers.

"I'm always going to love you." She brushed his nose with hers.

"Is that a promise?" His voice cracked.

"It is." She leaned back and waited for him to look at her again. When he did, she nodded. "In good times or in bad, whatever may come, I give you my word as well as my heart. Bennett Crofton, I will love you and honor you all the days of my life."

With a soft cry, Bennett wrapped his arms around her.

Now, finally, they had found their beginning.

THE END

(for now . . .)

I HOPE YOU'VE ENJOYED this return to Luna, Montana in this fourth book in Redemption Shores! Would you please leave an honest review to let other readers know what you think? Thank you!

Whew! It looks like Bennett and Hazel are FINALLY ready to step into their happily ever after! Big sigh of relief, right? And more, Hazel knows Jesus! That's the best.

But I'll bet you've still got questions. ;) Like, will we get to see an Elk Lake wedding? And what's going to happen to Gemma and

Nathan? And how about Isa, is she going to cause trouble in Luna? And why is Grady being . . . weird?

There are more stories to be told in Luna.

Keep watching for the release of those books.

While you're waiting, allow me to invite you to meet the Murphy Brothers—seven men forging their way through life and love, gripping faith, and learning to walk with God through all things. Theirs are stories of romance, but also of redemption. This nine book series is complete and ready for you to binge-read! Start book one today. :)

Made in the USA
Columbia, SC
22 July 2024

39141252R00140